Gambara

Honoré de Balzac

Translated by Clara Bell and James Waring

DEDICATION

To Monsieur le Marquis de Belloy

It was sitting by the fire, in a mysterious and magnificent retreat,—now a thing of the past but surviving in our memory,—whence our eyes commanded a view of Paris from the heights of Belleville to those of Belleville, from Montmartre to the triumphal Arc de l'Etoile, that one morning, refreshed by tea, amid the myriad suggestions that shoot up and die like rockets from your sparkling flow of talk, lavish of ideas, you tossed to my pen a figure worthy of Hoffmann,—that casket of unrecognized gems, that pilgrim seated at the gate of Paradise with ears to hear the songs of the angels but no longer a tongue to repeat them, playing on the ivory keys with fingers crippled by the stress of divine inspiration, believing that he is expressing celestial music to his bewildered listeners.

It was you who created GAMBARA; I have only clothed him. Let me render unto Caesar the things that are Caesar's, regretting only that you do not yourself take up the pen at a time when gentlemen ought to wield it as well as the sword, if they are to save their country. You may neglect yourself, but you owe your talents to us.

Gambara

New Year's Day of 1831 was pouring out its packets of sugared almonds, four o'clock was striking, there was a mob in the Palais-Royal, and the eating-houses were beginning to fill. At this moment a coupe drew up at the *perron* and a young man stepped out; a man of haughty appearance, and no doubt a foreigner; otherwise he would not have displayed the aristocratic *chasseur* who attended him in a plumed hat, nor the coat of arms which the heroes of July still attacked.

This gentleman went into the Palais-Royal, and followed the crowd round the galleries, unamazed at the slowness to which the throng of loungers reduced his pace; he seemed accustomed to the stately step which is ironically nicknamed the ambassador's strut; still, his dignity had a touch of the theatrical. Though his features were handsome and imposing, his hat, from beneath which thick black curls stood out, was perhaps tilted a little too much over the right ear, and belied his gravity by a too rakish effect. His eyes, inattentive and half closed, looked down disdainfully on the crowd.

"There goes a remarkably good-looking young man," said a girl in a low voice, as she made way for him to pass.

"And who is only too well aware of it!" replied her companion aloud —who was very plain.

After walking all round the arcades, the young man looked by turns at the sky and at his watch, and with a shrug of impatience went into a tobacconist's shop, lighted a cigar, and placed himself in front of a looking-glass to glance at his costume, which was rather more ornate than the rules of French taste allow. He pulled down his collar and his black velvet waistcoat, over which hung many festoons of the thick gold chain that is made at Venice; then, having arranged the folds of his cloak by a single jerk of his left shoulder, draping it gracefully so as to show the velvet lining, he started again on parade, indifferent to the glances of the vulgar.

As soon as the shops were lighted up and the dusk seemed to him black enough, he went out into the square in front of the Palais-Royal, but as a man anxious not to be recognized; for he kept close under the houses as far as the fountain, screened by the hackney-cab stand, till he reached the Rue Froid-Manteau, a dirty, poky, disreputable street —a sort of sewer tolerated by the police close to the purified purlieus of the Palais-Royal, as an Italian major-domo allows a careless servant to leave the sweepings of the rooms in a corner of the staircase.

The young man hesitated. He might have been a bedizened citizen's wife craning her neck over a gutter swollen by the rain. But the hour was not unpropitious for the indulgence of some discreditable whim. Earlier, he might have been detected; later, he might find himself cut out. Tempted by a glance which is encouraging without being inviting, to have followed a young and pretty woman for an hour, or perhaps for a day, thinking of her as a divinity and excusing her light conduct by a thousand reasons to her advantage; to have allowed oneself to believe in a sudden and irresistible affinity; to have pictured, under the promptings of transient excitement, a love-adventure in an age when romances are written precisely because they never happen; to have dreamed of balconies, guitars, stratagems, and bolts, enwrapped in Almaviva's cloak; and, after inditing a poem in fancy, to stop at the door of a house of ill-fame, and, crowning all, to discern in Rosina's bashfulness a reticence imposed by the police—is not all this, I say, an experience familiar to many a man who would not own it?

The most natural feelings are those we are least willing to confess, and among them is fatuity. When the lesson is carried no further, the Parisian profits by it, or forgets it, and no great harm is done. But this would hardly be the case with this foreigner, who was beginning to think he might pay too dearly for his Paris education.

This personage was a Milanese of good family, exiled from his native country, where some "liberal" pranks had made him an object of suspicion to the Austrian Government. Count Andrea Marcosini had been welcomed in Paris with the cordiality, essentially French, that a man always finds there, when he has a pleasant wit, a sounding name, two hundred thousand francs a year, and a prepossessing person. To such a man banishment could but be a pleasure tour; his property was simply sequestrated, and his friends let him know that after an absence of two years he might return to his native land without danger.

After rhyming *crudeli affanni* with *i miei tiranni* in a dozen or so of sonnets, and maintaining as many hapless Italian refugees out of his own purse, Count Andrea, who was so unlucky as to be a poet, thought himself released from patriotic obligations. So, ever since his arrival, he had given himself up recklessly to the pleasures of every kind which Paris offers *gratis* to those who can pay for them. His talents and his handsome person won him success among women, whom he adored collectively as beseemed his years, but among whom he had not as yet distinguished a chosen one. And indeed this taste was, in him, subordinate to those for music and poetry which he had cultivated from his childhood; and he thought success in these both more difficult and more glorious to achieve than in affairs of gallantry, since nature had not inflicted on him the obstacles men take most pride in defying.

A man, like many another, of complex nature, he was easily fascinated by the comfort of luxury, without which he could hardly have lived; and, in the same way, he clung to the social distinctions which his principles contemned. Thus his theories as an artist, a thinker, and a poet were in frequent antagonism with his tastes, his feelings, and his habits as a man of rank and wealth; but he comforted himself for his inconsistencies by recognizing them in many Parisians, like himself liberal by policy and aristocrats by nature.

Hence it was not without some uneasiness that he found himself, on December 31, 1830, under a Paris thaw, following at the heels of a woman whose dress betrayed the most abject, inveterate, and long-accustomed poverty, who was no handsomer than a hundred others to be seen any evening at the play, at the opera, in the world of fashion, and who was certainly not so young as Madame de Manerville, from whom he had obtained an assignation for that very day, and who was perhaps waiting for him at that very hour.

But in the glance at once tender and wild, swift and deep, which that woman's black eyes had shot at him by stealth, there was such a world of buried sorrows and promised joys! And she had colored so fiercely when, on coming out of a shop where she had lingered a quarter of an hour, her look frankly met the Count's, who had been waiting for her hard by! In fact, there were so many *buts* and *ifs*, that,

3

possessed by one of those mad temptations for which there is no word in any language, not even in that of the orgy, he had set out in pursuit of this woman, hunting her down like a hardened Parisian.

On the way, whether he kept behind or ahead of this damsel, he studied every detail of her person and her dress, hoping to dislodge the insane and ridiculous fancy that had taken up an abode in his brain; but he presently found in his examination a keener pleasure than he had felt only the day before in gazing at the perfect shape of a woman he loved, as she took her bath. Now and again, the unknown fair, bending her head, gave him a look like that of a kid tethered with its head to the ground, and finding herself still the object of his pursuit, she hurried on as if to fly. Nevertheless, each time that a block of carriages, or any other delay, brought Andrea to her side, he saw her turn away from his gaze without any signs of annoyance. These signals of restrained feelings spurred the frenzied dreams that had run away with him, and he gave them the rein as far as the Rue Froid-Manteau, down which, after many windings, the damsel vanished, thinking she had thus spoilt the scent of her pursuer, who was, in fact, startled by this move.

It was now quite dark. Two women, tattooed with rouge, who were drinking black-currant liqueur at a grocer's counter, saw the young woman and called her. She paused at the door of the shop, replied in a few soft words to the cordial greeting offered her, and went on her way. Andrea, who was behind her, saw her turn into one of the darkest yards out of this street, of which he did not know the name. The repulsive appearance of the house where the heroine of his romance had been swallowed up made him feel sick. He drew back a step to study the neighborhood, and finding an ill-looking man at his elbow, he asked him for information. The man, who held a knotted stick in his right hand, placed the left on his hip and replied in a single word:

"Scoundrel!"

But on looking at the Italian, who stood in the light of a street-lamp, he assumed a servile expression.

"I beg your pardon, sir," said he, suddenly changing his tone. "There is a restaurant near this, a sort of table-d'hote, where the cooking is pretty bad and they serve cheese in the soup. Monsieur is in search of the place, perhaps, for it is easy to see that he is an Italian —

Italians are fond of velvet and of cheese. But if monsieur would like to know of a better eating-house, an aunt of mine, who lives a few steps off, is very fond of foreigners."

Andrea raised his cloak as high as his moustache, and fled from the street, spurred by the disgust he felt at this foul person, whose clothes and manner were in harmony with the squalid house into which the fair unknown had vanished. He returned with rapture to the thousand luxuries of his own rooms, and spent the evening at the Marquise d'Espard's to cleanse himself, if possible, of the smirch left by the fancy that had driven him so relentlessly during the day.

And yet, when he was in bed, the vision came back to him, but clearer and brighter than the reality. The girl was walking in front of him; now and again as she stepped across a gutter her skirts revealed a round calf; her shapely hips swayed as she walked. Again Andrea longed to speak to her—and he dared not, he, Marcosini, a Milanese nobleman! Then he saw her turn into the dark passage where she had eluded him, and blamed himself for not having followed her.

"For, after all," said he to himself, "if she really wished to avoid me and put me off her track, it is because she loves me. With women of that stamp, coyness is a proof of love. Well, if I had carried the adventure any further, it would, perhaps, have ended in disgust. I will sleep in peace."

The Count was in the habit of analyzing his keenest sensations, as men do involuntarily when they have as much brains as heart, and he was surprised when he saw the strange damsel of the Rue Froid-Manteau once more, not in the pictured splendor of his dream but in the bare reality of dreary fact. And, in spite of it all, if fancy had stripped the woman of her livery of misery, it would have spoilt her for him; for he wanted her, he longed for her, he loved her—with her muddy stockings, her slipshod feet, her straw bonnet! He wanted her in the very house where he had seen her go in.

"Am I bewitched by vice, then?" he asked himself in dismay. "Nay, I have not yet reached that point. I am but three-and-twenty, and there is nothing of the senile fop about me."

The very vehemence of the whim that held possession of him to some extent reassured him. This strange struggle, these reflections, and this love in pursuit may perhaps puzzle some persons who are accustomed to the ways of Paris life; but they may be reminded that Count Andrea Marcosini was not a Frenchman.

Brought up by two abbes, who, in obedience to a very pious father, had rarely let him out of their sight, Andrea had not fallen in love with a cousin at the age of eleven, or seduced his mother's maid by the time he was twelve; he had not studied at school, where a lad does not learn only, or best, the subjects prescribed by the State; he had lived in Paris but a few years, and he was still open to those sudden but deep impressions against which French education and manners are so strong a protection. In southern lands a great passion is often born of a glance. A gentleman of Gascony who had tempered strong feelings by much reflection had fortified himself by many little recipes against sudden apoplexies of taste and heart, and he advised the Count to indulge at least once a month in a wild orgy to avert those storms of the soul which, but for such precautions, are apt to break out at inappropriate moments. Andrea now remembered this advice.

"Well," thought he, "I will begin to-morrow, January 1st."

This explains why Count Andrea Marcosini hovered so shyly before turning down the Rue Froid-Manteau. The man of fashion hampered the lover, and he hesitated for some time; but after a final appeal to his courage he went on with a firm step as far as the house, which he recognized without difficulty.

There he stopped once more. Was the woman really what he fancied her? Was he not on the verge of some false move?

At this juncture he remembered the Italian table d'hote, and at once jumped at the middle course, which would serve the ends alike of his curiosity and of his reputation. He went in to dine, and made his way down the passage; at the bottom, after feeling about for some time, he found a staircase with damp, slippery steps, such as to an Italian nobleman could only seem a ladder.

Invited to the first floor by the glimmer of a lamp and a strong smell of cooking, he pushed a door which stood ajar and saw a room dingy with dirt and smoke, where a wench was busy laying a table for about twenty customers. None of the guests had yet arrived.

After looking round the dimly lighted room where the paper was dropping in rags from the walls, the gentleman seated himself by a stove which was roaring and smoking in the corner.

Attracted by the noise the Count made in coming in and disposing of his cloak, the major-domo presently appeared. Picture to yourself a lean, dried-up cook, very tall, with a nose of extravagant dimensions, casting about him from time to time, with feverish keenness, a glance that he meant to be cautious. On seeing Andrea, whose attire bespoke considerable affluence, Signor Giardini bowed respectfully.

The Count expressed his intention of taking his meals as a rule in the society of some of his fellow-countrymen; he paid in advance for a certain number of tickets, and ingenuously gave the conversation a familiar bent to enable him to achieve his purpose quickly.

Hardly had he mentioned the woman he was seeking when Signor Giardini, with a grotesque shrug, looked knowingly at his customer, a bland smile on his lips.

"*Basta!*" he exclaimed. "*Capisco.* Your Excellency has come spurred by two appetites. La Signora Gambara will not have wasted her time if she has gained the interest of a gentleman so generous as you appear to be. I can tell you in a few words all we know of the woman, who is really to be pitied.

"The husband is, I believe, a native of Cremona and has just come here from Germany. He was hoping to get the Tedeschi to try some new music and some new instruments. Isn't it pitiable?" said Giardini, shrugging his shoulders. "Signor Gambara, who thinks himself a great composer, does not seem to me very clever in other ways. An excellent fellow with some sense and wit, and sometimes very agreeable, especially when he has had a few glasses of wine— which does not often happen, for he is desperately poor; night and day he toils at imaginary symphonies and operas instead of trying to earn an honest living. His poor wife is reduced to working for all sorts of people—the women on the streets! What is to be said? She loves her husband like a father, and takes care of him like a child.

"Many a young man has dined here to pay his court to madame; but not one has succeeded," said he, emphasizing the word. "La Signora Marianna is an honest woman, monsieur, much too honest, worse luck for her! Men give nothing for nothing nowadays. So the poor soul will die in harness.

"And do you suppose that her husband rewards her for her devotion? Pooh, my lord never gives her a smile! And all their cooking is done at the baker's; for not only does the wretched man never earn a sou; he spends all his wife can make on instruments which he carves, and lengthens, and shortens, and sets up and takes to pieces again till they produce sounds that will scare a cat; then he is happy. And yet you will find him the mildest, the gentlest of men. And, he is not idle; he is always at it. What is to be said? He is crazy and does not know his business. I have seen him, monsieur, filing and forging his instruments and eating black bread with an appetite that I envied him —I, who have the best table in Paris.

"Yes, Excellenza, in a quarter of an hour you shall know the man I am. I have introduced certain refinements into Italian cookery that will amaze you! Excellenza, I am a Neapolitan—that is to say, a born cook. But of what use is instinct without knowledge? Knowledge! I have spent thirty years in acquiring it, and you see where it has left me. My history is that of every man of talent. My attempts, my experiments, have ruined three restaurants in succession at Naples, Parma, and Rome. To this day, when I am reduced to make a trade of my art, I more often than not give way to my ruling passion. I give these poor refugees some of my choicest dishes. I ruin myself! Folly! you will say? I know it; but how can I help it? Genius carries me away, and I cannot resist concocting a dish which smiles on my fancy.

"And they always know it, the rascals! They know, I can promise you, whether I or my wife has stood over the fire. And what is the consequence? Of sixty-odd customers whom I used to see at my table every day when I first started in this wretched place, I now see twenty on an average, and give them credit for the most part. The Piedmontese, the Savoyards, have deserted, but the connoisseurs, the true Italians, remain. And there is no sacrifice that I would not make for them. I often give them a dinner for five and twenty sous which has cost me double."

Signore Giardini's speech had such a full flavor of Neapolitan cunning that the Count was delighted, and could have fancied himself at Gerolamo's.

"Since that is the case, my good friend," said he familiarly to the cook, "and since chance and your confidence have let me into the secret of your daily sacrifices, allow me to pay double."

As he spoke Andrea spun a forty-franc piece on the stove, out of which Giardini solemnly gave him two francs and fifty centimes in change, not without a certain ceremonious mystery that amused him hugely.

"In a few minutes now," the man added, "you will see your *donnina*. I will seat you next the husband, and if you wish to stand in his good graces, talk about music. I have invited every one for the evening, poor things. Being New Year's Day, I am treating the company to a dish in which I believe I have surpassed myself."

Signor Giardini's voice was drowned by the noisy greetings of the guests, who streamed in two and two, or one at a time, after the manner of tables-d'hote. Giardini stayed by the Count, playing the showman by telling him who the company were. He tried by his witticisms to bring a smile to the lips of a man who, as his Neapolitan instinct told him, might be a wealthy patron to turn to good account.

"This one," said he, "is a poor composer who would like to rise from song-writing to opera, and cannot. He blames the managers, music-sellers,—everybody, in fact, but himself, and he has no worse enemy. You can see—what a florid complexion, what self-conceit, how little firmness in his features! he is made to write ballads. The man who is with him and looks like a match-hawker, is a great music celebrity— Gigelmi, the greatest Italian conductor known; but he has gone deaf, and is ending his days in penury, deprived of all that made it tolerable. Ah! here comes our great Ottoboni, the most guileless old fellow on earth; but he is suspected of being the most vindictive of all who are plotting for the regeneration of Italy. I cannot think how they can bear to banish such a good man."

And here Giardini looked narrowly at the Count, who, feeling himself under inquisition as to his politics, entrenched himself in Italian impassibility.

"A man whose business it is to cook for all comers can have no political opinions, Excellenza," Giardini went on. "But to see that worthy man, who looks more like a lamb than a lion, everybody

9

would say what I say, were it before the Austrian ambassador himself. Besides, in these times liberty is no longer proscribed; it is going its rounds again. At least, so these good people think," said he, leaning over to speak in the Count's ear, "and why should I thwart their hopes? I, for my part, do not hate an absolute government. Excellenza, every man of talent is for depotism!

"Well, though full of genius, Ottoboni takes no end of pains to educate Italy; he writes little books to enlighten the intelligence of the children and the common people, and he smuggles them very cleverly into Italy. He takes immense trouble to reform the moral sense of our luckless country, which, after all, prefers pleasure to freedom,—and perhaps it is right."

The Count preserved such an impenetrable attitude that the cook could discover nothing of his political views.

"Ottoboni," he ran on, "is a saint; very kind-hearted; all the refugees are fond of him; for, Excellenza, a liberal may have his virtues. Oho! Here comes a journalist," said Giardini, as a man came in dressed in the absurd way which used to be attributed to a poet in a garret; his coat was threadbare, his boots split, his hat shiny, and his overcoat deplorably ancient. "Excellenza, that poor man is full of talent, and incorruptibly honest. He was born into the wrong times, for he tells the truth to everybody; no one can endure him. He writes theatrical articles for two small papers, though he is clever enough to work for the great dailies. Poor fellow!

"The rest are not worth mentioning, and Your Excellency will find them out," he concluded, seeing that on the entrance of the musician's wife the Count had ceased to listen to him.

On seeing Andrea here, Signora Marianna started visibly and a bright flush tinged her cheeks.

"Here he is!" said Giardini, in an undertone, clutching the Count's arm and nodding to a tall man. "How pale and grave he is poor man! His hobby has not trotted to his mind to-day, I fancy."

Andrea's prepossession for Marianna was crossed by the captivating charm which Gambara could not fail to exert over every genuine artist. The composer was now forty; but although his high brow was bald and lined with a few parallel, but not deep, wrinkles; in spite, too, of hollow temples where the blue veins showed through the smooth, transparent skin, and of the deep sockets in which his black eyes were sunk, with their large lids and light lashes, the lower part of his face made him still look young, so calm was its outline, so soft the modeling. It could be seen at a glance that in this man passion had been curbed to the advantage of the intellect; that the brain alone had grown old in some great struggle.

Andrea shot a swift look at Marianna, who was watching him. And he noted the beautiful Italian head, the exquisite proportion and rich coloring that revealed one of those organizations in which every human power is harmoniously balanced, he sounded the gulf that divided this couple, brought together by fate. Well content with the promise he inferred from this dissimilarity between the husband and wife, he made no attempt to control a liking which ought to have raised a barrier between the fair Marianna and himself. He was already conscious of feeling a sort of respectful pity for this man, whose only joy she was, as he understood the dignified and serene acceptance of ill fortune that was expressed in Gambara's mild and melancholy gaze.

After expecting to see one of the grotesque figures so often set before us by German novelists and writers of *libretti*, he beheld a simple, unpretentious man, whose manners and demeanor were in nothing strange and did not lack dignity. Without the faintest trace of luxury, his dress was more decent than might have been expected from his extreme poverty, and his linen bore witness to the tender care which watched over every detail of his existence. Andrea looked at Marianna with moistened eyes; and she did not color, but half smiled, in a way that betrayed, perhaps, some pride at this speechless homage. The Count, too thoroughly fascinated to miss the smallest indication of complaisance, fancied that she must love him, since she understood him so well.

From this moment he set himself to conquer the husband rather than the wife, turning all his batteries against the poor Gambara, who quite guilelessly went on eating Signor Giardini's *bocconi*, without thinking of their flavor.

The Count opened the conversation on some trivial subject, but at the first words he perceived that this brain, supposed to be infatuated on one point, was remarkably clear on all others, and saw that it would be far more important to enter into this very clever man's ideas than to flatter his conceits.

The rest of the company, a hungry crew whose brain only responded to the sight of a more or less good meal, showed much animosity to the luckless Gambara, and waited only till the end of the first course, to give free vent to their satire. A refugee, whose frequent leer betrayed ambitious schemes on Marianna, and who fancied he could establish himself in her good graces by trying to make her husband ridiculous, opened fire to show the newcomer how the land lay at the table-d'hote.

"It is a very long time since we have heard anything about the opera on 'Mahomet'!" cried he, with a smile at Marianna. "Can it be that Paolo Gambara, wholly given up to domestic cares, absorbed by the charms of the chimney-corner, is neglecting his superhuman genius, leaving his talents to get cold and his imagination to go flat?"

Gambara knew all the company; he dwelt in a sphere so far above them all that he no longer cared to repel an attack. He made no reply.

"It is not given to everybody," said the journalist, "to have an intellect that can understand Monsieur Gambara's musical efforts, and that, no doubt, is why our divine maestro hesitates to come before the worthy Parisian public."

"And yet," said the ballad-monger, who had not opened his mouth but to swallow everything that came within his reach, "I know some men of talent who think highly of the judgments of Parisian critics. I myself have a pretty reputation as a musician," he went on, with an air of diffidence. "I owe it solely to my little songs in *vaudevilles*, and the success of my dance music in drawing-rooms; but I propose ere long to bring out a mass composed for the anniversary of Beethoven's death, and I expect to be better appreciated in Paris than anywhere else. You will perhaps do me the honor of hearing it?" he said, turning to Andrea.

"Thank you," said the Count. "But I do not conceive that I am gifted with the organs needful for the appreciation of French music. If you were dead, monsieur, and Beethoven had composed the mass, I would not have failed to attend the performance."

This retort put an end to the tactics of those who wanted to set Gambara off on his high horse to amuse the new guest. Andrea was already conscious of an unwillingness to expose so noble and pathetic a mania as a spectacle for so much vulgar shrewdness. It was with no base reservation that he kept up a desultory conversation, in the course of which Signor Giardini's nose not infrequently interposed between two remarks. Whenever Gambara uttered some elegant repartee or some paradoxical aphorism, the cook put his head forward, to glance with pity at the musician and with meaning at the Count, muttering in his ear, "*E matto!*"

Then came a moment when the *chef* interrupted the flow of his judicial observations to devote himself to the second course, which he considered highly important. During his absence, which was brief, Gambara leaned across to address Andrea.

"Our worthy host," said he, in an undertone, "threatens to regale us to-day with a dish of his own concocting, which I recommend you to avoid, though his wife has had an eye on him. The good man has a mania for innovations. He ruined himself by experiments, the last of which compelled him to fly from Rome without a passport—a circumstance he does not talk about. After purchasing the good-will of a popular restaurant he was trusted to prepare a banquet given by a lately made Cardinal, whose household was not yet complete. Giardini fancied he had an opportunity for distinguishing himself— and he succeeded! for that same evening he was accused of trying to poison the whole conclave, and was obliged to leave Rome and Italy without waiting to pack up. This disaster was the last straw. Now," and Gambara put his finger to his forehead and shook his head.

"He is a good fellow, all the same," he added. "My wife will tell you that we owe him many a good turn."

Giardini now came in carefully bearing a dish which he set in the middle of the table, and he then modestly resumed his seat next to Andrea, whom he served first. As soon as he had tasted the mess, the Count felt that an impassable gulf divided the second mouthful from the first. He was much embarrassed, and very anxious not to annoy the cook, who was watching him narrowly. Though a French *restaurateur* may care little about seeing a dish scorned if he is sure of being paid for it, it is not so with an Italian, who is not often satiated with praises.

To gain time, Andrea complimented Giardini enthusiastically, but he leaned over to whisper in his ear, and slipping a gold piece into his hand under the table, begged him to go out and buy a few bottles of champagne, leaving him free to take all the credit of the treat.

When the Italian returned, every plate was cleared, and the room rang with praises of the master-cook. The champagne soon mounted these southern brains, and the conversation, till now subdued in the stranger's presence, overleaped the limits of suspicious reserve to wander far over the wide fields of political and artistic opinions.

Andrea, to whom no form of intoxication was known but those of love and poetry, had soon gained the attention of the company and skilfully led it to a discussion of matters musical.

"Will you tell me, monsieur," said he to the composer of dance-music, "how it is that the Napoleon of these tunes can condescend to usurp the place of Palestrina, Pergolesi, and Mozart,—poor creatures who must pack and vanish at the advent of that tremendous Mass for the Dead?"

"Well, monsieur," replied the composer, "a musician always finds it difficult to reply when the answer needs the cooperation of a hundred skilled executants. Mozart, Haydn, and Beethoven, without an orchestra would be of no great account."

"Of no great account!" said Marcosini. "Why, all the world knows that the immortal author of *Don Giovanni* and the *Requiem* was named Mozart; and I am so unhappy as not to know the name of the inexhaustible writer of quadrilles which are so popular in our drawing-rooms—"

"Music exists independently of execution," said the retired conductor, who, in spite of his deafness, had caught a few words of the conversation. "As he looks through the C-minor symphony by Beethoven, a musician is transported to the world of fancy on the golden wings of the subject in G-natural repeated by the horns in E. He sees a whole realm, by turns glorious in dazzling shafts of light, gloomy under clouds of melancholy, and cheered by heavenly strains."

"The new school has left Beethoven far behind," said the ballad-writer, scornfully.

"Beethoven is not yet understood," said the Count. "How can he be excelled?"

Gambara drank a large glass of champagne, accompanying the draught by a covert smile of approval.

"Beethoven," the Count went on, "extended the limits of instrumental music, and no one followed in his track."

Gambara assented with a nod.

"His work is especially noteworthy for simplicity of construction and for the way the scheme is worked out," the Count went on. "Most composers make use of the orchestral parts in a vague, incoherent way, combining them for a merely temporary effect; they do not persistently contribute to the whole mass of the movement by their steady and regular progress. Beethoven assigns its part to each tone-quality from the first. Like the various companies which, by their disciplined movements, contribute to winning a battle, the orchestral parts of a symphony by Beethoven obey the plan ordered for the interest of all, and are subordinate to an admirably conceived scheme.

"In this he may be compared to a genius of a different type. In Walter Scott's splendid historical novels, some personage, who seems to have least to do with the action of the story, intervenes at a given moment and leads up to the climax by some thread woven into the plot."

"*E vero!*" remarked Gambara, to whom common sense seemed to return in inverse proportion to sobriety.

Andrea, eager to carry the test further, for a moment forgot all his predilections; he proceeded to attack the European fame of Rossini, disputing the position which the Italian school has taken by storm, night after night for more than thirty years, on a hundred stages in Europe. He had undertaken a hard task. The first words he spoke raised a strong murmur of disapproval; but neither the repeated interruptions, nor exclamations, nor frowns, nor contemptuous looks, could check this determined advocate of Beethoven.

"Compare," said he, "that sublime composer's works with what by common consent is called Italian music. What feebleness of ideas, what limpness of style! That monotony of form, those commonplace cadenzas, those endless bravura passages introduced at haphazard irrespective of the dramatic situation, that recurrent *crescendo* that Rossini brought into vogue, are now an integral part of every composition; those vocal fireworks result in a sort of babbling, chattering, vaporous mucic, of which the sole merit depends on the greater or less fluency of the singer and his rapidity of vocalization.

"The Italian school has lost sight of the high mission of art. Instead of elevating the crowd, it has condescended to the crowd; it has won its success only by accepting the suffrages of all comers, and appealing to the vulgar minds which constitute the majority. Such a success is mere street juggling.

"In short, the compositions of Rossini, in whom this music is personified, with those of the writers who are more or less of his school, to me seem worthy at best to collect a crowd in the street round a grinding organ, as an accompaniment to the capers of a puppet show. I even prefer French music, and I can say no more. Long live German music!" cried he, "when it is tuneful," he added to a low voice.

This sally was the upshot of a long preliminary discussion, in which, for more than a quarter of an hour, Andrea had divagated in the upper sphere of metaphysics, with the ease of a somnambulist walking over the roofs.

Gambara, keenly interested in all this transcendentalism, had not lost a word; he took up his parable as soon as Andrea seemed to have ended, and a little stir of revived attention was evident among the guests, of whom several had been about to leave.

"You attack the Italian school with much vigor," said Gambara, somewhat warmed to his work by the champagne, "and, for my part, you are very welcome. I, thank God, stand outside this more or less melodic frippery. Still, as a man of the world, you are too ungrateful to the classic land whence Germany and France derived their first teaching. While the compositions of Carissimi, Cavalli, Scarlatti, and Rossi were being played throughout Italy, the violin players of the Paris opera house enjoyed the singular privilege of being allowed to play in gloves. Lulli, who extended the realm of harmony, and was the first to classify discords, on arriving in France found but two men —a cook and a mason—whose voice and intelligence were equal to performing his music; he made a tenor of the former, and transformed the latter into a bass. At that time Germany had no musician excepting Sebastian Bach.—But you, monsieur, though you are so young," Gambara added, in the humble tone of a man who expects to find his remarks received with scorn or ill-nature, "must have given much time to the study of these high matters of art; you could not otherwise explain them so clearly."

This word made many of the hearers smile, for they had understood nothing of the fine distinctions drawn by Andrea. Giardini, indeed, convinced that the Count had been talking mere rhodomontade, nudged him with a laugh in his sleeve, as at a good joke in which he flattered himself that he was a partner.

"There is a great deal that strikes me as very true in all you have said," Gambara went on; "but be careful. Your argument, while reflecting on Italian sensuality, seems to me to lean towards German idealism, which is no less fatal heresy. If men of imagination and good sense, like you, desert one camp only to join the other; if they cannot keep to the happy medium between two forms of extravagance, we shall always be exposed to the satire of the sophists, who deny all progress, who compare the genius of man to this tablecloth, which, being too short to cover the whole of Signor Giardini's table, decks one end at the expense of the other."

Giardini bounded in his seat as if he had been stung by a horse-fly, but swift reflections restored him to his dignity as a host; he looked up to heaven and again nudged the Count, who was beginning to think the cook more crazy than Gambara.

This serious and pious way of speaking of art interested the Milanese extremely. Seated between these two distracted brains, one so noble and the other so common, and making game of each other to the great entertainment of the crowd, there was a moment when the Count found himself wavering between the sublime and its parody, the farcical extremes of human life. Ignoring the chain of incredible events which had brought them to this smoky den, he believed himself to be the plaything of some strange hallucination, and thought of Gambara and Giardini as two abstractions.

Meanwhile, after a last piece of buffoonery from the deaf conductor in reply to Gambara, the company had broken up laughing loudly. Giardini went off to make coffee, which he begged the select few to accept, and his wife cleared the table. The Count, sitting near the stove between Marianna and Gambara, was in the very position which the mad musician thought most desirable, with sensuousness on one side and idealism on the other. Gambara finding himself for the first time in the society of a man who did not laugh at him to his face, soon diverged from generalities to talk of himself, of his life, his work, and the musical regeneration of which he believed himself to be the Messiah.

"Listen," said he, "you who so far have not insulted me. I will tell you the story of my life; not to make a boast of my perseverance, which is no virtue of mine, but to the greater glory of Him who has given me strength. You seem kind and pious; if you do not believe in me at least you will pity me. Pity is human; faith comes from God."

Andrea turned and drew back under his chair the foot that had been seeking that of the fair Marianna, fixing his eyes on her while listening to Gambara.

"I was born at Cremona, the son of an instrument maker, a fairly good performer and an even better composer," the musician began. "Thus at an early age I had mastered the laws of musical construction in its twofold aspects, the material and the spiritual; and as an inquisitive child I observed many things which subsequently recurred to the mind of the full-grown man.

"The French turned us out of our own home—my father and me. We were ruined by the war. Thus, at the age of ten I entered on the wandering life to which most men have been condemned whose brains were busy with innovations, whether in art, science, or politics. Fate, or the instincts of their mind which cannot fit into the compartments where the trading class sit, providentially guides them to the spots where they may find teaching. Led by my passion for music I wandered throughout Italy from theatre to theatre, living on very little, as men can live there. Sometimes I played the bass in an orchestra, sometimes I was on the boards in the chorus, sometimes under them with the carpenters. Thus I learned every kind of musical effect, studying the tones of instruments and of the human voice, wherein they differed and how they harmonized, listening to the score and applying the rules taught me by my father.

"It was hungry work, in a land where the sun always shines, where art is all pervading, but where there is no pay for the artist, since

Rome is but nominally the Sovereign of the Christian world. Sometimes made welcome, sometimes scouted for my poverty, I never lost courage. I heard a voice within me promising me fame.

"Music seemed to me in its infancy, and I think so still. All that is left to us of musical effort before the seventeenth century, proves to me that early musicians knew melody only; they were ignorant of harmony and its immense resources. Music is at once a science and an art. It is rooted in physics and mathematics, hence it is a science; inspiration makes it an art, unconsciously utilizing the theorems of science. It is founded in physics by the very nature of the matter it works on. Sound is air in motion. The air is formed of constituents which, in us, no doubt, meet with analogous elements that respond to them, sympathize, and magnify them by the power of the mind. Thus the air must include a vast variety of molecules of various degrees of elasticity, and capable of vibrating in as many different periods as there are tones from all kinds of sonorous bodies; and these molecules, set in motion by the musician and falling on our ear, answer to our ideas, according to each man's temperament. I myself believe that sound is identical in its nature with light. Sound is light, perceived under another form; each acts through vibrations to which man is sensitive and which he transforms, in the nervous centres, into ideas.

"Music, like painting, makes use of materials which have the property of liberating this or that property from the surrounding medium and so suggesting an image. The instruments in music perform this part, as color does in painting. And whereas each sound produced by a sonorous body is invariably allied with its major third and fifth, whereas it acts on grains of fine sand lying on stretched parchment so as to distribute them in geometrical figures that are always the same, according to the pitch,—quite regular when the combination is a true chord, and indefinite when the sounds are dissonant,—I say that music is an art conceived in the very bowels of nature.

"Music is subject to physical and mathematical laws. Physical laws are but little known, mathematics are well understood; and it is since their relations have been studied, that the harmony has been created to which we owe the works of Haydn, Mozart, Beethoven, and Rossini, grand geniuses, whose music is undoubtedly nearer to perfection than that of their precursors, though their genius, too, is unquestionable. The old masters could sing, but they had not art and science at their command,—a noble alliance which enables us to merge into one the finest melody and the power of harmony.

"Now, if a knowledge of mathematical laws gave us these four great musicians, what may we not attain to if we can discover the physical laws in virtue of which—grasp this clearly—we may collect, in larger or smaller quantities, according to the proportions we may require, an ethereal substance diffused in the atmosphere which is the medium alike of music and of light, of the phenomena of vegetation and of animal life! Do you follow me? Those new laws would arm the composer with new powers by supplying him with instruments superior of those now in use, and perhaps with a potency of harmony immense as compared with that now at his command. If every modified shade of sound answers to a force, that must be known to enable us to combine all these forces in accordance with their true laws.

"Composers work with substances of which they know nothing. Why should a brass and a wooden instrument—a bassoon and horn—have so little identity of tone, when they act on the same matter, the constituent gases of the air? Their differences proceed from some displacement of those constituents, from the way they act on the elements which are their affinity and which they return, modified by some occult and unknown process. If we knew what the process was, science and art would both be gainers. Whatever extends science enhances art.

"Well, these are the discoveries I have guessed and made. Yes," said Gambara, with increasing vehemence, "hitherto men have noted effects rather than causes. If they could but master the causes, music would be the greatest of the arts. Is it not the one which strikes deepest to the soul? You see in painting no more than it shows you; in poetry you have only what the poet says; music goes far beyond this. Does it not form your taste, and rouse dormant memories? In a concert-room there may be a thousand souls; a strain is flung out from Pasta's throat, the execution worthily answering to the ideas that flashed through Rossini's mind as he wrote the air. That phrase of Rossini's, transmitted to those attentive souls, is worked out in so many different poems. To one it presents a woman long dreamed of; to another, some distant shore where he wandered long ago. It rises up before him with its drooping willows, its clear waters, and the hopes that then played under its leafy arbors. One woman is reminded of the myriad feelings that tortured her during an hour of jealousy, while another thinks of the unsatisfied cravings of her heart, and paints in the glowing hues of a dream an ideal lover, to whom she abandons herself with the rapture of the woman in the Roman mosaic who embraces a chimera; yet a third is thinking that this very evening some hoped-for joy is to be hers, and rushes by anticipation into the tide of happiness, its dashing waves breaking against her burning bosom. Music alone has this power of throwing us back on ourselves; the other arts give us infinite pleasure. But I am digressing.

"These were my first ideas, vague indeed; for an inventor at the beginning only catches glimpses of the dawn, as it were. So I kept these glorious ideas at the bottom of my knapsack, and they gave me spirit to eat the dry crust I often dipped in the water of a spring. I worked, I composed airs, and, after playing them on any instrument that came to hand, I went off again on foot across Italy. Finally, at the age of two-and-twenty, I settled in Venice, where for the first time I enjoyed rest and found myself in a decent position. I there made the acquaintance of a Venetian nobleman who liked my ideas, who encouraged me in my investigations, and who got me employment at the Venice theatre.

"Living was cheap, lodging inexpensive. I had a room in that Capello palace from which the famous Bianca came forth one evening to become a Grand Duchess of Tuscany. And I would dream that my unrecognized fame would also emerge from thence one day to be crowned.

"I spent my evenings at the theatre and my days in work. Then came disaster. The performance of an opera in which I had experimented, trying my music, was a failure. No one understood my score for the *Martiri*. Set Beethoven before the Italians and they are out of their depth. No one had patience enough to wait for the effect to be produced by the different motives given out by each instrument, which were all at last to combine in a grand *ensemble*.

"I had built some hopes on the success of the *Martiri*, for we votaries of the blue divinity Hope always discount results. When a man believes himself destined to do great things, it is hard not to fancy them achieved; the bushel always has some cracks through which the light shines.

"My wife's family lodged in the same house, and the hope of winning Marianna, who often smiled at me from her window, had done much to encourage my efforts. I now fell into the deepest melancholy as I sounded the depths of a life of poverty, a perpetual struggle in which love must die. Marianna acted as genius does; she jumped across every obstacle, both feet at once. I will not speak of the little happiness which shed its gilding on the beginning of my misfortunes. Dismayed at my failure, I decided that Italy was not intelligent enough and too much sunk in the dull round of routine to accept the innovations I conceived of; so I thought of going to Germany.

"I traveled thither by way of Hungary, listening to the myriad voices of nature, and trying to reproduce that sublime harmony by the help of instruments which I constructed or altered for the purpose. These experiments involved me in vast expenses which had soon exhausted my savings. And yet those were our golden days. In Germany I was appreciated. There has been nothing in my life more glorious than that time. I can think of nothing to compare with the vehement joys I found by the side of Marianna, whose beauty was then of really heavenly radiance and splendor. In short, I was happy.

"During that period of weakness I more than once expressed my passion in the language of earthly harmony. I even wrote some of those airs, just like geometrical patterns, which are so much admired in the world of fashion that you move in. But as soon as I made a little way I met with insuperable obstacles raised by my rivals, all hypercritical or unappreciative.

"I had heard of France as being a country where novelties were favorably received, and I wanted to get there; my wife had a little money and we came to Paris. Till then no one had actually laughed in my face; but in this dreadful city I had to endure that new form of torture, to which abject poverty ere long added its bitter sufferings. Reduced to lodging in this mephitic quarter, for many months we have lived exclusively on Marianna's sewing, she having found employment for her needle in working for the unhappy prostitutes who make this street their hunting ground. Marianna assures me that among those poor creatures she has met with such consideration and generosity as I, for my part, ascribe to the ascendency of virtue so pure that even vice is compelled to respect it."

"Hope on," said Andrea. "Perhaps you have reached the end of your trials. And while waiting for the time when my endeavor, seconding yours, shall set your labors in a true light, allow me, as a fellow-countryman and an artist like yourself, to offer you some little advances on the undoubted success of your score."

"All that has to do with matters of material existence I leave to my wife," replied Gambara. "She will decide as to what we may accept without a blush from so thorough a gentleman as you seem to be. For my part,—and it is long since I have allowed myself to indulge such full confidences,—I must now ask you to allow me to leave you. I see a melody beckoning to me, dancing and floating before me, bare and quivering, like a girl entreating her lover for her clothes which he has hidden. Good-night. I must go and dress my mistress. My wife I leave with you."

He hurried away, as a man who blames himself for the loss of valuable time; and Marianna, somewhat embarrassed, prepared to follow him.

Andrea dared not detain her.

Giardini came to the rescue.

"But you heard, signora," said he. "Your husband has left you to settle some little matters with the Signor Conte."

Marianna sat down again, but without raising her eyes to Andrea, who hesitated before speaking.

"And will not Signor Gambara's confidence entitle me to his wife's?" he said in agitated tones. "Can the fair Marianna refuse to tell me the story of her life?"

"My life!" said Marianna. "It is the life of the ivy. If you wish to know the story of my heart, you must suppose me equally destitute of pride and of modesty if you can ask me to tell it after what you have just heard."

"Of whom, then, can I ask it?" cried the Count, in whom passion was blinding his wits.

"Of yourself," replied Marianna. "Either you understand me by this time, or you never will. Try to ask yourself."

"I will, but you must listen. And this hand, which I am holding, is to lie in mine as long as my narrative is truthful."

"I am listening," said Marianna.

"A woman's life begins with her first passion," said Andrea. "And my dear Marianna began to live only on the day when she first saw Paolo Gambara. She needed some deep passion to feed upon, and, above all, some interesting weakness to shelter and uphold. The beautiful woman's nature with which she is endowed is perhaps not so truly passion as maternal love.

"You sigh, Marianna? I have touched one of the aching wounds in your heart. It was a noble part for you to play, so young as you were, —that of protectress to a noble but wandering intellect. You said to yourself: 'Paolo will be my genius; I shall be his common sense; between us we shall be that almost divine being called an angel,— the sublime creature that enjoys and understands, reason never stifling love.'

"And then, in the first impetus of youth, you heard the thousand voices of nature which the poet longed to reproduce. Enthusiasm clutched you when Paolo spread before you the treasures of poetry, while seeking to embody them in the sublime but restricted language of music; you admired him when delirious rapture carried him up and away from you, for you liked to believe that all this devious energy would at last come down and alight as love. But you knew not the tyrannous and jealous despotism of the ideal over the minds that fall in love with it. Gambara, before meeting you, had given himself over to the haughty and overbearing mistress, with whom you have struggled for him to this day.

"Once, for an instant, you had a vision of happiness. Paolo, tumbling from the lofty sphere where his spirit was constantly soaring, was amazed to find reality so sweet; you fancied that his madness would be lulled in the arms of love. But before long Music again clutched her prey. The dazzling mirage which had cheated you into the joys of reciprocal love made the lonely path on which you had started look more desolate and barren.

"In the tale your husband has just told me, I could read, as plainly as in the contrast between your looks and his, all the painful secrets of that ill-assorted union, in which you have accepted the sufferer's part. Though your conduct has been unfailingly heroical, though your firmness has never once given way in the exercise of your painful duties, perhaps, in the silence of lonely nights, the heart that at this moment is beating so wildly in your breast, may, from time to time, have rebelled. Your husband's superiority was in itself your worst torment. If he had been less noble, less single-minded, you might have deserted him; but his virtues upheld yours; you wondered, perhaps, whether his heroism or your own would be the first to give way.

"You clung to your really magnanimous task as Paolo clung to his chimera. If you had had nothing but a devotion to duty to guide and sustain you, triumph might have seemed easier; you would only have had to crush your heart, and transfer your life into the world of abstractions; religion would have absorbed all else, and you would have lived for an idea, like those saintly women who kill all the instincts of nature at the foot of the altar. But the all-pervading charm of Paolo, the loftiness of his mind, his rare and touching proofs of tenderness, constantly drag you down from that ideal realm where virtue would fain maintain you; they perennially revive in you the energies you have exhausted in contending with the phantom of love. You never suspected this! The faintest glimmer of hope led you on in pursuit of the sweet vision.

"At last the disappointments of many years have undermined your patience,—an angel would have lost it long since,—and now the apparition so long pursued is no more than a shade without substance. Madness that is so nearly allied to genius can know no cure in this world. When this thought first struck you, you looked back on your past youth, sacrificed, if not wasted; you then bitterly discerned the blunder of nature that had given you a father when you looked for a husband. You asked yourself whether you had not gone beyond the duty of a wife in keeping yourself wholly for a man who was bound up in his science. Marianna, leave your hand in mine; all I have said is true. And you looked about you—but now you were in Paris, not in Italy, where men know how to love—"

"Oh! Let me finish the tale," cried Marianna. "I would rather say things myself. I will be honest; I feel that I am speaking to my truest friend. Yes, I was in Paris when all you have expressed so clearly took place in my mind; but when I saw you I was saved, for I had never met with the love I had dreamed of from my childhood. My poor dress and my dwelling-place had hidden me from the eyes of men of your class. A few young men, whose position did not allow of their insulting me, were all the more intolerable for the levity with which they treated me. Some made game of my husband, as if he were merely a ridiculous old man; others basely tried to win his good graces to betray me; one and all talked of getting me away from him, and none understood the devotion I feel for a soul that is so far away from us only because it is so near heaven, for that friend, that brother, whose handmaid I will always be.

"You alone understood, did you not? the tie that binds me to him. Tell me that you feel a sincere and disinterested regard for my Paolo—"

"I gladly accept your praises," Andrea interrupted; "but go no further; do not compel me to contradict you. I love you, Marianna, as we love in the beautiful country where we both were born, I love you with all my soul and with all my strength; but before offering you that love, I will be worthy of yours. I will make a last attempt to give back to you the man you have loved so long and will love forever. Till success or defeat is certain, accept without any shame the modest ease I can give you both. We will go to-morrow and choose a place where he may live.

"Have you such regard for me as will allow you to make me the partner in your guardianship?"

Marianna, surprised at such magnanimity, held out her hand to the Count, who went away, trying to evade the civilities of Giardini and his wife.

On the following day Giardini took the Count up to the room where the Gambaras lodged. Though Marianna fully knew her lover's noble soul, —for there are natures which quickly enter into each other's spirit, —Marianna was too good a housewife not to betray her annoyance at receiving such a fine gentleman in so humble a room. Everything was exquisitely clean. She had spent the morning in dusting her motley furniture, the handiwork of Signor Giardini, who had put it together, at odd moments of leisure, out of the fragments of the instruments rejected by Gambara.

Gambara

Andrea had never seen anything quite so crazy. To keep a decent countenance he turned away from a grotesque bed, contrived by the ingenious cook in the case of an old harpsichord, and looked at Marianna's narrow couch, of which the single mattress was covered with a white muslin counterpane, a circumstance that gave rise in his mind to some sad but sweet thoughts.

He wished to speak of his plans and of his morning's work; but Gambara, in his enthusiasm, believing that he had at last met with a willing listener, took possession of him, and compelled him to listen to the opera he had written for Paris.

"In the first place, monsieur," said the composer, "allow me to explain the subject in a few words. Here, the hearers receiving a musical impression do not work it out in themselves, as religion bids us work out the texts of Scripture in prayer. Hence it is very difficult to make them understand that there is in nature an eternal melody, exquisitely sweet, a perfect harmony, disturbed only by revolutions independent of the divine will, as passions are uncontrolled by the will of men.

"I, therefore, had to seek a vast framework in which effect and cause might both be included; for the aim of my music is to give a picture of the life of nations from the loftiest point of view. My opera, for which I myself wrote the *libretto*, for a poet would never have fully developed the subject, is the life of Mahomet,—a figure in whom the magic of Sabaeanism combined with the Oriental poetry of the Hebrew Scriptures to result in one of the greatest human epics, the Arab dominion. Mahomet certainly derived from the Hebrews the idea of a despotic government, and from the religion of the shepherd tribes or Sabaeans the spirit of expansion which created the splendid empire of the Khalifs. His destiny was stamped on him in his birth, for his father was a heathen and his mother a Jewess. Ah! my dear Count to be a great musician a man must be very learned. Without knowledge he can get no local color and put no ideas into his music. The composer who sings for singing's sake is an artisan, not an artist.

"This magnificent opera is the continuation of the great work I projected. My first opera was called *The Martyrs*, and I intend to write a third on Jerusalem delivered. You perceive the beauty of this trilogy and what a variety of motives it offers,—the Martyrs, Mahomet, the Deliverance of Jerusalem: the God of the West, the

27

God of the East, and the struggle of their worshipers over a tomb. But we will not dwell on my fame, now for ever lost.

"This is the argument of my opera." He paused. "The first act," he went on, "shows Mahomet as a porter to Kadijah, a rich widow with whom his uncle placed him. He is in love and ambitious. Driven from Mecca, he escapes to Medina, and dates his era from his flight, the *Hegira*. In the second act he is a Prophet, founding a militant religion. In the third, disgusted with all things, having exhausted life, Mahomet conceals the manner of his death in the hope of being regarded as a god,—last effort of human pride.

"Now you shall judge of my way of expressing in sound a great idea, for which poetry could find no adequate expression in words."

Gambara sat down to the piano with an absorbed gaze, and his wife brought him the mass of papers forming his score; but he did not open them.

"The whole opera," said he, "is founded on a bass, as on a fruitful soil. Mahomet was to have a majestic bass voice, and his wife necessarily had a contralto. Kadijah was quite old—twenty! Attention! This is the overture. It begins with an *andante* in C major, triple time. Do you hear the sadness of the ambitious man who is not satisfied with love? Then, through his lamentation, by a transition to the key of E flat, *allegro*, common time, we hear the cries of the epileptic lover, his fury and certain warlike phrases, for the mighty charms of the one and only woman give him the impulse to multiplied loves which strikes us in *Don Giovanni*. Now, as you hear these themes, do you not catch a glimpse of Mahomet's Paradise?

"And next we have a *cantabile* (A flat major, six-eight time), that might expand the soul that is least susceptible to music. Kadijah has understood Mahomet! Then Kadijah announces to the populace the Prophet's interviews with the Angel Gabriel (*maestoso sostenuto* in F Major). The magistrates and priests, power and religion, feeling themselves attacked by the innovator, as Christ and Socrates also attacked effete or worn-out powers and religions, persecute Mahomet and drive him out of Mecca (*stretto* in C major). Then comes my beautiful dominant (G major, common time). Arabia now harkens to the Prophet; horsemen arrive (G major, E flat, B flat, G minor, and still common time). The mass of men gathers like an avalanche; the false Prophet has begun on a tribe the work he will achieve over a world (G major).

"He promises the Arabs universal dominion, and they believe him because he is inspired. The *crescendo* begins (still in the dominant). Here come some flourishes (in C major) from the brass, founded on the harmony, but strongly marked, and asserting themselves as an expression of the first triumphs. Medina has gone over to the Prophet, and the whole army marches on Mecca (an explosion of sound in C major). The whole power of the orchestra is worked up like a conflagration; every instrument is employed; it is a torrent of harmony.

"Suddenly the *tutti* is interrupted by a flowing air (on the minor third). You hear the last strain of devoted love. The woman who had upheld the great man dies concealing her despair, dies at the moment of triumph for him in whom love has become too overbearing to be content with one woman; and she worships him enough to sacrifice herself to the greatness of the man who is killing her. What a blaze of love!

"Then the Desert rises to overrun the world (back to C major). The whole strength of the orchestra comes in again, collected in a tremendous quintet grounded on the fundamental bass—and he is dying! Mahomet is world-weary; he has exhausted everything. Now he craves to die a god. Arabia, in fact, worships and prays to him, and we return to the first melancholy strain (C minor) to which the curtain rose.

"Now, do you not discern," said Gambara, ceasing to play, and turning to the Count, "in this picturesque and vivid music—abrupt, grotesque, or melancholy, but always grand—the complete expression of the life of an epileptic, mad for enjoyment, unable to read or write, using all his defects as stepping-stones, turning every blunder and disaster into a triumph? Did not you feel a sense of his fascination exerted over a greedy and lustful race, in this overture, which is an epitome of the opera?"

At first calm and stern, the maestro's face, in which Andrea had been trying to read the ideas he was uttering in inspired tones, though the chaotic flood of notes afforded no clue to them, had by degrees glowed with fire and assumed an impassioned force that infected Marianna and the cook. Marianna, too, deeply affected by certain passages in which she recognized a picture of her own position, could not conceal the expression of her eyes from Andrea.

Gambara wiped his brow, and shot a glance at the ceiling of such fierce energy that he seemed to pierce it and soar to the very skies.

"You have seen the vestibule," said he; "we will now enter the palace. The opera begins:—

"Act I. Mahomet, alone on the stage, begins with an air (F natural, common time), interrupted by a chorus of camel-drivers gathered round a well at the back of the stage (they sing in contrary time — twelve-eight). What majestic woe! It will appeal to the most frivolous women, piercing to their inmost nerves if they have no heart. Is not this the very expression of crushed genius?"

To Andrea's great astonishment,—for Marianna was accustomed to it, —Gambara contracted his larynx to such a pitch that the only sound was a stifled cry not unlike the bark of a watch-dog that has lost its voice. A slight foam came to the composer's lips and made Andrea shudder.

"His wife appears (A minor). Such a magnificent duet! In this number I have shown that Mahomet has the will and his wife the brains. Kadijah announces that she is about to devote herself to an enterprise that will rob her of her young husband's love. Mahomet means to conquer the world; this his wife has guessed, and she supports him by persuading the people of Mecca that her husband's attacks of epilepsy are the effect of his intercourse with the angels (chorus of the first followers of Mahomet, who come to promise him their aid, C sharp minor, *sotto voce*). Mahomet goes off to seek the Angel Gabriel (*recitative* in F major). His wife encourages the disciples (*aria*, interrupted by the chorus, gusts of chanting support Kadijah's broad and majestic air, A major).

"Abdallah, the father of Ayesha,—the only maiden Mahomet has found really innocent, wherefore he changed the name of Abdallah to Abubekir (the father of the virgin),—comes forward with Ayesha and sings against the chorus, in strains which rise above the other voices and supplement the air sung by Kadijah in contrapuntal treatment. Omar, the father of another maiden who is to be Mahomet's concubine, follows Abubekir's example; he and his daughter join in to form a quintette. The girl Ayesha is first soprano, Hafsa second soprano; Abubekir is a bass, Omar a baritone.

"Mahomet returns, inspired. He sings his first *bravura* air, the beginning of the *finale* (E major), promising the empire of the world to those who believe in him. The Prophet seeing the two damsels, then, by a gentle transition (from B major to G major), addresses them in amorous tones. Ali, Mahomet's cousin, and Khaled, his greatest general, both tenors, now arrive and announce the persecution; the magistrates, the military, and the authorities have all proscribed the Prophet (*recitative*). Mahomet declares in an invocation (in C) that the Angel Gabriel is on his side, and points to a pigeon that is seen flying away. The chorus of believers responds in accents of devotion (on a modulation to B major). The soldiers, magistrates, and officials then come on (*tempo di marcia*, common time, B major). A chorus in two divisions (*stretto* in E major). Mahomet yields to the storm (in a descending phrase of diminished sevenths) and makes his escape. The fierce and gloomy tone of this *finale* is relieved by the phrases given to the three women who foretell Mahomet's triumph, and these motives are further developed in the third act in the scene where Mahomet is enjoying his splendor."

The tears rose to Gambara's eyes, and it was only upon controlling his emotion that he went on.

"Act II. The religion is now established. The Arabs are guarding the Prophet's tent while he speaks with God (chorus in A minor). Mahomet appears (a prayer in F). What a majestic and noble strain is this that forms the bass of the voices, in which I have perhaps enlarged the borders of melody. It was needful to express the wonderful energy of this great human movement which created an architecture, a music, a poetry of its own, a costume and manners. As you listen, you are walking under the arcades of the Generalife, the carved vaults of the Alhambra. The runs and trills depict that delicate mauresque decoration, and the gallant and valorous religion which was destined to wage war against the gallant and valorous chivalry of Christendom. A few brass instruments awake in the orchestra, announcing the Prophet's first triumph (in a broken *cadenza*). The Arabs adore the Prophet (E flat major), and the Khaled, Amru, and Ali arrive (*tempo di marcia*). The armies of the faithful have taken many towns and subjugated the three Arabias. Such a grand recitative!—Mahomet rewards his generals by presenting them with maidens.

"And here," said Gambara, sadly, "there is one of those wretched ballets, which interrupt the thread of the finest musical tragedies! But Mahomet elevates it once more by his great prophetic scene, which poor Monsieur Voltaire begins with these words:

"Arabia's time at last has come!

"He is interrupted by a chorus of triumphant Arabs (twelve-eight time, *accelerando*). The tribes arrive in crowds; the horns and brass reappear in the orchestra. General rejoicings ensue, all the voices joining in by degrees, and Mahomet announces polygamy. In the midst of all this triumph, the woman who has been of such faithful service to Mahomet sings a magnificent air (in B major). 'And I,' says she, 'am I no longer loved?' 'We must part. Thou art but a woman, and I am a Prophet; I may still have slaves but no equal.' Just listen to this duet (G sharp minor). What anguish! The woman understands the greatness her hands have built up; she loves Mahomet well enough to sacrifice herself to his glory; she worships him as a god, without criticising him,—without murmuring. Poor woman! His first dupe and his first victim!

"What a subject for the *finale* (in B major) is her grief, brought out in such sombre hues against the acclamations of the chorus, and mingling with Mahomet's tones as he throws his wife aside as a tool of no further use, still showing her that he can never forget her! What fireworks of triumph! what a rush of glad and rippling song go up from the two young voices (first and second soprano) of Ayesha and Hafsa, supported by Ali and his wife, by Omar and Abubekir! Weep!—rejoice! —Triumph and tears! Such is life."

Marianna could not control her tears, and Andrea was so deeply moved that his eyes were moist. The Neapolitan cook was startled by the magnetic influence of the ideas expressed by Gambara's convulsive accents.

The composer looked round, saw the group, and smiled.

"At last you understand me!" said he.

No conqueror, led in pomp to the Capitol under the purple beams of glory, as the crown was placed on his head amid the acclamations of a nation, ever wore such an expression. The composer's face was radiant, like that of a holy martyr. No one dispelled the error. A terrible smile parted Marianna's lips. The Count was appalled by the guilelessness of this mania.

"Act III," said the enchanted musician, reseating himself at the piano. "(*Andantino, solo.*) Mahomet in his seraglio, surrounded by women, but not happy. Quartette of Houris (A major). What pompous harmony, what trills as of ecstatic nightingales! Modulation (into F sharp minor). The theme is stated (on the dominant E and repeated in F major). Here every delight is grouped and expressed to give effect to the contrast of the gloomy *finale* of the first act. After the dancing, Mahomet rises and sings a grand *bravura* air (in F minor), repelling the perfect and devoted love of his first wife, but confessing himself conquered by polygamy. Never has a musician had so fine a subject! The orchestra and the chorus of female voices express the joys of the Houris, while Mahomet reverts to the melancholy strain of the opening. Where is Beethoven," cried Gambara, "to appreciate this prodigious reaction of my opera on itself? How completely it all rests on the bass.

"It is thus that Beethoven composed his E minor symphony. But his heroic work is purely instrumental, whereas here, my heroic phrase is worked out on a sextette of the finest human voices, and a chorus of the faithful on guard at the door of the sacred dwelling. I have every resource of melody and harmony at my command, an orchestra and voices. Listen to the utterance of all these phases of human life, rich and poor;—battle, triumph, and exhaustion!

"Ali arrives, the Koran prevails in every province (duet in D minor). Mahomet places himself in the hands of his two fathers-in-law; he will abdicate his rule and die in retirement to consolidate his work. A magnificent sextette (B flat major). He takes leave of all (solo in F natural). His two fathers-in-law, constituted his vicars or Khalifs, appeal to the people. A great triumphal march, and a prayer by all the Arabs kneeling before the sacred house, the Kasbah, from which a pigeon is seen to fly away (the same key). This prayer, sung by sixty voices and led by the women (in B flat), crowns the stupendous work expressive of the life of nations and of man. Here you have every emotion, human and divine."

Andrea gazed at Gambara in blank amazement. Though at first he had been struck by the terrible irony of the situation,—this man expressing the feelings of Mahomet's wife without discovering them in Marianna,—the husband's hallucination was as nothing compared with the composer's. There was no hint even of a poetical or musical idea in the hideous cacophony with which he had deluged their ears; the first principles of harmony, the most elementary rules of composition, were absolutely alien to this chaotic structure. Instead of the scientifically compacted music which Gambara described, his fingers produced sequences of fifths, sevenths, and octaves, of major thirds, progressions of fourths with no supporting bass,—a medley of discordant sounds struck out haphazard in such a way as to be excruciating to the least sensitive ear. It is difficult to give any idea of the grotesque performance. New words would be needed to describe this impossible music.

Andrea, painfully affected by this worthy man's madness, colored, and stole a glance at Marianna; while she, turning pale and looking down, could not restrain her tears. In the midst of this chaos of notes, Gambara had every now and then given vent to his rapture in exclamations of delight. He had closed his eyes in ecstasy; had smiled at his piano; had looked at it with a frown; put out his tongue at it after the fashion of the inspired performer,—in short, was quite intoxicated with the poetry that filled his brain, and that he had vainly striven to utter. The strange discords that clashed under his fingers had obviously sounded in his ears like celestial harmonies.

A deaf man, seeing the inspired gaze of his blue eyes open on another world, the rosy glow that tinged his cheeks, and, above all, the heavenly serenity which ecstasy stamped on his proud and noble countenance, would have supposed that he was looking on at the improvisation of a really great artist. The illusion would have been all the more natural because the performance of this mad music required immense executive skill to achieve such fingering. Gambara must have worked at it for years.

Nor were his hands alone employed; his feet were constantly at work with complicated pedaling; his body swayed to and fro; the perspiration poured down his face while he toiled to produce a great *crescendo* with the feeble means the thankless instrument placed at his command. He stamped, puffed, shouted; his fingers were as swift as the serpent's double tongue; and finally, at the last crash on the keys, he fell back in his chair, resting his head on the top of it.

"*Per Bacco!* I am quite stunned," said the Count as he left the house. "A child dancing on the keyboard would make better music."

"Certainly mere chance could not more successfully avoid hitting two notes in concord than that possessed creature has done during the past hour," said Giardini.

"How is it that the regular beauty of Marianna's features is not spoiled by incessantly hearing such a hideous medley?" said the Count to himself. "Marianna will certainly grow ugly."

"Signor, she must be saved from that," cried Giardini.

"Yes," said Andrea. "I have thought of that. Still, to be sure that my plans are not based on error, I must confirm my doubts by another experiment. I will return and examine the instruments he has invented. To-morrow, after dinner, we will have a little supper. I will send in some wine and little dishes."

The cook bowed.

Andrea spent the following day in superintending the arrangement of the rooms where he meant to install the artist in a humble home.

In the evening the Count made his appearance, and found the wine, according to his instructions, set out with some care by Marianna and Giardini. Gambara proudly exhibited the little drums, on which lay the powder by means of which he made his observations on the pitch and quality of the sounds emitted by his instruments.

"You see," said he, "by what simple means I can prove the most important propositions. Acoustics thus can show me the analogous effects of sound on every object of its impact. All harmonies start from a common centre and preserve the closest relations among themselves; or rather, harmony, like light, is decomposable by our art as a ray is by a prism."

He then displayed the instruments constructed in accordance with his laws, explaining the changes he had introduced into their constitution. And finally he announced that to conclude this preliminary inspection, which could only satisfy a superficial curiosity, he would perform on an instrument that contained all the elements of a complete orchestra, and which he called a *Panharmonicon*.

"If it is the machine in that huge case, which brings down on us the complaints of the neighborhood whenever you work at it, you will not play on it long," said Giardini. "The police will interfere. Remember that!"

"If that poor idiot stays in the room," said Gambara in a whisper to the Count, "I cannot possibly play."

Andrea dismissed the cook, promising a handsome reward if he would keep watch outside and hinder the neighbors or the police from interfering. Giardini, who had not stinted himself while helping Gambara to wine, was quite willing.

Gambara, without being drunk, was in the condition when every power of the brain is over-wrought; when the walls of the room are transparent; when the garret has no roof, and the soul soars in the empyrean of spirits.

Marianna, with some little difficulty, removed the covers from an instrument as large as a grand piano, but with an upper case added. This strange-looking instrument, besides this second body and its keyboard, supported the openings or bells of various wind instruments and the closed funnels of a few organ pipes.

"Will you play me the prayer you say is so fine at the end of your opera?" said the Count.

To the great surprise of both Marianna and the Count, Gambara began with a succession of chords that proclaimed him a master; and their astonishment gave way first to amazed admiration and then to perfect rapture, effacing all thought of the place and the performer. The effects of a real orchestra could not have been finer than the voices of the wind instruments, which were like those of an organ and combined wonderfully with the harmonies of the strings. But the unfinished condition of the machine set limits to the composer's execution, and his idea seemed all the greater; for, often, the very perfection of a work of art limits its suggestiveness to the recipient soul. Is not this proved by the preference accorded to a sketch rather than a finished picture when on their trial before those who interpret a work in their own mind rather than accept it rounded off and complete?

The purest and serenest music that Andrea had ever listened to rose up from under Gambara's fingers like the vapor of incense from an altar. The composer's voice grew young again, and, far from marring the noble melody, it elucidated it, supported it, guided it,—just as the feeble and quavering voice of an accomplished reader, such as Andrieux, for instance, can expand the meaning of some great scene by Corneille or Racine by lending personal and poetical feeling.

This really angelic strain showed what treasures lay hidden in that stupendous opera, which, however, would never find comprehension so long as the musician persisted in trying to explain it in his present demented state. His wife and the Count were equally divided between the music and their surprise at this hundred-voiced instrument, inside which a stranger might have fancied an invisible chorus of girls were hidden, so closely did some of the tones resemble the human voice; and they dared not express their ideas by a look or a word. Marianna's face was lighted up by a radiant beam of hope which revived the glories of her youth. This renascence of beauty, co-existent with the luminous glow of her husband's genius, cast a shade of regret on the Count's exquisite pleasure in this mysterious hour.

"You are our good genius!" whispered Marianna. "I am tempted to believe that you actually inspire him; for I, who never am away from him, have never heard anything like this."

"And Kadijah's farewell!" cried Gambara, who sang the *cavatina* which he had described the day before as sublime, and which now brought tears to the eyes of the lovers, so perfectly did it express the loftiest devotion of love.

"Who can have taught you such strains?" cried the Count.

"The Spirit," said Gambara. "When he appears, all is fire. I see the melodies there before me; lovely, fresh in vivid hues like flowers. They beam on me, they ring out,—and I listen. But it takes a long, long time to reproduce them."

"Some more!" said Marianna.

Gambara, who could not tire, played on without effort or antics. He performed his overture with such skill, bringing out such rich and original musical effects, that the Count was quite dazzled, and at last believed in some magic like that commanded by Paganini and Liszt, —a style of execution which changes every aspect of music as an art, by giving it a poetic quality far above musical inventions.

"Well, Excellenza, and can you cure him?" asked Giardini, as Andrea came out.

"I shall soon find out," replied the Count. "This man's intellect has two windows; one is closed to the world, the other is open to the heavens. The first is music, the second is poetry. Till now he has insisted on sitting in front of the shuttered window; he must be got to the other. It was you, Giardini, who first started me on the right track, by telling me that your client's mind was clearer after drinking a few glasses of wine."

"Yes," cried the cook, "and I can see what your plan is."

"If it is not too late to make the thunder of poetry audible to his ears, in the midst of the harmonies of some noble music, we must put him into a condition to receive it and appreciate it. Will you help me to intoxicate Gambara, my good fellow? Will you be none the worse for it?"

"What do you mean, Excellenza?"

Andrea went off without answering him, laughing at the acumen still left to this cracked wit.

On the following day he called for Marianna, who had spent the morning in arranging her dress,—a simple but decent outfit, on which she had spent all her little savings. The transformation would have destroyed the illusions of a mere dangler; but Andrea's caprice had become a passion. Marianna, diverted of her picturesque poverty, and looking like any ordinary woman of modest rank, inspired dreams of wedded life.

He handed her into a hackney coach, and told her of the plans he had in his head; and she approved of everything, happy in finding her admirer more lofty, more generous, more disinterested than she had dared to hope. He took her to a little apartment, where he had allowed himself to remind her of his good offices by some of the elegant trifles which have a charm for the most virtuous women.

"I will never speak to you of love till you give up all hope of your Paolo," said the Count to Marianna, as he bid her good-bye at the Rue Froid-Manteau. "You will be witness to the sincerity of my attempts. If they succeed. I may find myself unequal to keeping up my part as a friend; but in that case I shall go far away, Marianna. Though I have firmness enough to work for your happiness, I shall not have so much as will enable me to look on at it."

"Do not say such things. Generosity, too, has its dangers," said she, swallowing down her tears. "But are you going now?"

"Yes," said Andrea; "be happy, without any drawbacks."

If Giardini might be believed, the new treatment was beneficial to both husband and wife. Every evening after his wine, Gambara seemed less self-centered, talked more, and with great lucidity; he even spoke at last of reading the papers. Andrea could not help quaking at his unexpectedly rapid success; but though his distress made him aware of the strength of his passion, it did not make him waver in his virtuous resolve.

One day he called to note the progress of this singular cure. Though the state of the patient at first gave him satisfaction, his joy was dashed by Marianna's beauty, for an easy life had restored its brilliancy. He called now every evening to enjoy calm and serious conversation, to which he contributed lucid and well considered arguments controverting Gambara's singular theories. He took advantage of the remarkable acumen of the composer's mind as to every point not too directly bearing on his manias, to obtain his assent to principles in various branches of art, and apply them subsequently to music. All was well so long as the patient's brain was heated with the fumes of wine; but as soon as he had recovered—or, rather, lost—his reason, he was a monomaniac once more.

However, Paolo was already more easily diverted by the impression of outside things; his mind was more capable of addressing itself to several points at a time.

Andrea, who took an artistic interest in his semi-medical treatment, thought at last that the time had come for a great experiment. He would give a dinner at his own house, to which he would invite Giardini for the sake of keeping the tragedy and the parody side by side, and afterwards take the party to the first performance of *Robert le Diable*. He had seen it in rehearsal, and he judged it well fitted to open his patient's eyes.

By the end of the second course, Gambara was already tipsy, laughing at himself with a very good grace; while Giardini confessed that his culinary innovations were not worth a rush. Andrea had neglected nothing that could contribute to this twofold miracle. The wines of Orvieto and of Montefiascone, conveyed with the peculiar care needed in moving them, Lachrymachristi and Giro,—all the heady liqueurs of *la cara Patria*,—went to their brains with the intoxication alike of the grape and of fond memory. At dessert the musician and the cook both abjured every heresy; one was humming a *cavatina* by Rossini, and the other piling delicacies on his plate and washing them down with Maraschino from Zara, to the prosperity of the French *cuisine*.

The Count took advantage of this happy frame of mind, and Gambara allowed himself to be taken to the opera like a lamb.

At the first introductory notes Gambara's intoxication appeared to clear away and make way for the feverish excitement which sometimes brought his judgment and his imagination into perfect harmony; for it was their habitual disagreement, no doubt, that caused his madness. The ruling idea of that great musical drama appeared to him, no doubt, in its noble simplicity, like a lightning flash, illuminating the utter darkness in which he lived. To his unsealed eyes this music revealed the immense horizons of a world in which he found himself for the first time, though recognizing it as that he had seen in his dreams. He fancied himself transported into the scenery of his native land, where that beautiful Italian landscape begins at what Napoleon so cleverly described as the *glacis* of the Alps. Carried back by memory to the time when his young and eager brain was as yet untroubled by the ecstasy of his too exuberant imagination he listened with religious awe and would not utter a single word. The Count respected the internal travail of his soul. Till half-past twelve Gambara sat so perfectly motionless that the frequenters of the opera house took him, no doubt, for what he was—a man drunk.

On their return, Andrea began to attack Meyerbeer's work, in order to wake up Gambara, who sat sunk in the half-torpid state common in drunkards.

"What is there in that incoherent score to reduce you to a condition of somnambulism?" asked Andrea, when they got out at his house. "The story of *Robert le Diable*, to be sure, is not devoid of interest, and Holtei has worked it out with great skill in a drama that is very well written and full of strong and pathetic situations; but the French librettist has contrived to extract from it the most ridiculous farrago of nonsense. The absurdities of the libretti of Vesari and Schikander are not to compare with those of the words of Robert le Diable; it is a dramatic nightmare, which oppresses the hearer without deeply moving him.

"And Meyerbeer has given the devil a too prominent part. Bertram and Alice represent the contest between right and wrong, the spirits of good and evil. This antagonism offered a splendid opportunity to the composer. The sweetest melodies, in juxtaposition with harsh and crude strains, was the natural outcome of the form of the story; but in the German composer's score the demons sing better than the saints. The heavenly airs belie their origin, and when the composer abandons the infernal motives he returns to them as soon as possible, fatigued with the effort of keeping aloof from them. Melody, the golden thread that ought never to be lost throughout so vast a plan, often vanishes from Meyerbeer's work. Feeling counts for nothing, the heart has no part in it. Hence we never come upon those happy inventions, those artless scenes, which captivate all our sympathies and leave a blissful impression on the soul.

"Harmony reigns supreme, instead of being the foundation from which the melodic groups of the musical picture stand forth. These discordant combinations, far from moving the listener, arouse in him a feeling analogous to that which he would experience on seeing a rope-dancer hanging to a thread and swaying between life and death. Never does a soothing strain come in to mitigate the fatiguing suspense. It really is as though the composer had had no other object in view than to produce a baroque effect without troubling himself about musical truth or unity, or about the capabilities of human voices which are swamped by this flood of instrumental noise."

"Silence, my friend!" cried Gambara. "I am still under the spell of that glorious chorus of hell, made still more terrible by the long trumpets,—a new method of instrumentation. The broken *cadenzas* which give such force to Robert's scene, the *cavatina* in the fourth act, the *finale* of the first, all hold me in the grip of a supernatural power. No, not even Gluck's declamation ever produced so prodigious an effect, and I am amazed by such skill and learning."

"Signor Maestro," said Andrea, smiling, "allow me to contradict you. Gluck, before he wrote, reflected long; he calculated the chances, and he decided on a plan which might be subsequently modified by his inspirations as to detail, but hindered him from ever losing his way. Hence his power of emphasis, his declamatory style thrilling with life and truth. I quite agree with you that Meyerbeer's learning is transcendent; but science is a defect when it evicts inspiration, and it seems to me that we have in this opera the painful toil of a refined craftsman who in his music has but picked up thousands of phrases out of other operas, damned or forgotten, and appropriated them, while extending, modifying, or condensing them. But he has fallen into the error of all selectors of *centos*,—an abuse of good things. This clever harvester of notes is lavish of discords, which, when too often introduced, fatigue the ear till those great effects pall upon it which a composer should husband with care to make the more effective use of them when the situation requires it. These enharmonic passages recur to satiety, and the abuse of the plagal cadence deprives it of its religious solemnity.

"I know, of course, that every musician has certain forms to which he drifts back in spite of himself; he should watch himself so as to avoid that blunder. A picture in which there were no colors but blue and red would be untrue to nature, and fatigue the eye. And thus the constantly recurring rhythm in the score of *Robert le Diable* makes the work, as a whole, appear monotonous. As to the effect of the long trumpets, of which you speak, it has long been known in Germany; and what Meyerbeer offers us as a novelty was constantly used by Mozart, who gives just such a chorus to the devils in *Don Giovanni*."

By plying Gambara, meanwhile, with fresh libations, Andrea thus strove, by his contradictoriness, to bring the musician back to a true sense of music, by proving to him that his so-called mission was not to try to regenerate an art beyond his powers, but to seek to express himself in another form; namely, that of poetry.

"But, my dear Count, you have understood nothing of that stupendous musical drama," said Gambara, airily, as standing in front of Andrea's piano he struck the keys, listened to the tone, and then seated himself, meditating for a few minutes as if to collect his ideas.

"To begin with, you must know," said he, "that an ear as practised as mine at once detected that labor of choice and setting of which you spoke. Yes, the music has been selected, lovingly, from the storehouse of a rich and fertile imagination wherein learning has squeezed every idea to extract the very essence of music. I will illustrate the process."

He rose to carry the candles into the adjoining room, and before sitting down again he drank a full glass of Giro, a Sardinian wine, as full of fire as the old wines of Tokay can inspire.

"Now, you see," said Gambara, "this music is not written for misbelievers, nor for those who know not love. If you have never suffered from the virulent attacks of an evil spirit who shifts your object just as you are taking aim, who puts a fatal end to your highest hopes,—in one word, if you have never felt the devil's tail whisking over the world, the opera of *Robert le Diable* must be to you, what the Apocalypse is to those who believe that all things will end with them. But if, persecuted and wretched, you understand that Spirit of Evil,—the monstrous ape who is perpetually employed in destroying the work of God,—if you can conceive of him as having, not indeed loved, but ravished, an almost divine woman, and achieved through her the joy of paternity; as so loving his son that he would rather have him eternally miserable with himself than think of him as eternally happy with God; if, finally, you can imagine the mother's soul for ever hovering over the child's head to snatch it from the atrocious temptations offered by its father,—even then you will have but a faint idea of this stupendous drama, which needs but little to make it worthy of comparison with Mozart's *Don Giovanni*. *Don Giovanni* is in its perfection the greater, I grant; *Robert le Diable* expresses ideas, *Don Giovanni* arouses sensations. *Don Giovanni* is as yet the only musical work in which harmony and melody are combined in exactly the right proportions. In this lies its only superiority, for *Robert* is the richer work. But how vain are such comparisons since each is so beautiful in its own way!

"To me, suffering as I do from the demon's repeated shocks, Robert spoke with greater power than to you; it struck me as being at the same time vast and concentrated.

"Thanks to you, I have been transported to the glorious land of dreams where our senses expand, and the world works on a scale which is gigantic as compared with man."

He was silent for a space.

"I am trembling still," said the ill-starred artist, "from the four bars of cymbals which pierced to my marrow as they opened that short, abrupt introduction with its solo for trombone, its flutes, oboes, and clarionet, all suggesting the most fantastic effects of color. The *andante* in C minor is a foretaste of the subject of the evocation of the ghosts in the abbey, and gives grandeur to the scene by anticipating the spiritual struggle. I shivered."

Gambara pressed the keys with a firm hand and expanded Meyerbeer's theme in a masterly *fantasia*, a sort of outpouring of his soul after the manner of Liszt. It was no longer the piano, it was a whole orchestra that they heard; the very genius of music rose before them.

"That was worthy of Mozart!" he exclaimed. "See how that German can handle his chords, and through what masterly modulations he raises the image of terror to come to the dominant C. I can hear all hell in it!

"The curtain rises. What do I see? The only scene to which we gave the epithet infernal: an orgy of knights in Sicily. In that chorus in F every human passion is unchained in a bacchanalian *allegro*. Every thread by which the devil holds us is pulled. Yes, that is the sort of glee that comes over men when they dance on the edge of a precipice; they make themselves giddy. What *go* there is in that chorus!

"Against that chorus—the reality of life—the simple life of every-day virtue stands out in the air, in G minor, sung by Raimbaut. For a moment it refreshed my spirit to hear the simple fellow, representative of verdurous and fruitful Normandy, which he brings to Robert's mind in the midst of his drunkenness. The sweet influence of his beloved native land lends a touch of tender color to this gloomy opening.

"Then comes the wonderful air in C major, supported by the chorus in C minor, so expressive of the subject. '*Je suis Robert!*' he immediately breaks out. The wrath of the prince, insulted by his vassal, is already more than natural anger; but it will die away, for memories of his childhood come to him, with Alice, in the bright and graceful *allegro* in A major.

"Can you not hear the cries of the innocent dragged into this infernal drama,—a persecuted creature? *'Non, non,'*" sang Gambara, who made the consumptive piano sing. "His native land and tender emotions have come back to him; his childhood and its memories have blossomed anew in Robert's heart. And now his mother's shade rises up, bringing with it soothing religious thoughts. It is religion that lives in that beautiful song in E major, with its wonderful harmonic and melodic progression in the words:

> "Car dans les cieux, comme sur la terre,
> Sa mere va prier pour lui.

"Here the struggle begins between the unseen powers and the only human being who has the fire of hell in his veins to enable him to resist them; and to make this quite clear, as Bertram comes on, the great musician has given the orchestra a passage introducing a reminiscence of Raimbaut's ballad. What a stroke of art! What cohesion of all the parts! What solidity of structure!

"The devil is there, in hiding, but restless. The conflict of the antagonistic powers opens with Alice's terror; she recognizes the devil of the image of Saint Michael in her village. The musical subject is worked out through an endless variety of phases. The antithesis indispensable in opera is emphatically presented in a noble *recitative*, such as a Gluck might have composed, between Bertram and Robert:

> "Tu se sauras jamais a quel exces je t'aime.

"In that diabolical C minor, Bertram, with his terrible bass, begins his work of undermining which will overthrow every effort of the vehement, passionate man.

"Here, everything is appalling. Will the crime get possession of the criminal? Will the executioner seize his victim? Will sorrow consume the artist's genius? Will the disease kill the patient? or, will the guardian angel save the Christian?

"Then comes the *finale*, the gambling scene in which Bertram tortures his son by rousing him to tremendous emotions. Robert, beggared, frenzied, searching everything, eager for blood, fire, and sword, is his own son; in this mood he is exactly like his father. What hideous glee we hear in Bertram's words: '*Je ris de tes coups!*' And how perfectly the Venetian *barcarole* comes in here. Through what wonderful transitions the diabolical parent is brought on to the stage once more to make Robert throw the dice.

"This first act is overwhelming to any one capable of working out the subjects in his very heart, and lending them the breadth of development which the composer intended them to call forth.

"Nothing but love could now be contrasted with this noble symphony of song, in which you will detect no monotony, no repetitions of means and effects. It is one, but many; the characteristic of all that is truly great and natural.

"I breathe more freely; I find myself in the elegant circle of a gallant court; I hear Isabella's charming phrases, fresh, but almost melancholy, and the female chorus in two divisions, and in *imitation*, with a suggestion of the Moorish coloring of Spain. Here the terrifying music is softened to gentler hues, like a storm dying away, and ends in the florid prettiness of a duet wholly unlike anything that has come before it. After the turmoil of a camp full of errant heroes, we have a picture of love. Poet! I thank thee! My heart could not have borne much more. If I could not here and there pluck the daisies of a French light opera, if I could not hear the gentle wit of a woman able to love and to charm, I could not endure the terrible deep note on which Bertram comes in, saying to his son: '*Si je la permets!*' when Robert had promised the princess he adores that he will conquer with the arms she has bestowed on him.

"The hopes of the gambler cured by love, the love of a most beautiful woman,—did you observe that magnificent Sicilian, with her hawk's eye secure of her prey? (What interpreters that composer has found!) the hopes of the man are mocked at by the hopes of hell in the tremendous cry: '*A toi, Robert de Normandie!*'

"And are not you struck by the gloom and horror of those long-held notes, to which the words are set: '*Dans la foret prochaine*'? We find here all the sinister spells of *Jerusalem Delivered*, just as we find all chivalry in the chorus with the Spanish lilt, and in the march tune.

How original is the *alegro* with the modulations of the four cymbals (tuned to C, D, C, G)! How elegant is the call to the lists! The whole movement of the heroic life of the period is there: the mind enters into it; I read in it a romance, a poem of chivalry. The *exposition* is now finished; the resources of music would seem to be exhausted; you have never heard anything like it before; and yet it is homogeneous. You have had life set before you, and its one and only *crux*: 'Shall I be happy or unhappy?' is the philosopher's query. 'Shall I be saved or damned?' asks the Christian."

With these words Gambara struck the last chord of the chorus, dwelt on it with a melancholy modulation, and then rose to drink another large glass of Giro. This half-African vintage gave his face a deeper flush, for his passionate and wonderful sketch of Meyerbeer's opera had made him turn a little pale.

"That nothing may be lacking to this composition," he went on, "the great artist has generously added the only *buffo* duet permissible for a devil: that in which he tempts the unhappy troubadour. The composer has set jocosity side by side with horror—a jocosity in which he mocks at the only realism he had allowed himself amid the sublime imaginings of his work—the pure calm love of Alice and Raimbaut; and their life is overshadowed by the forecast of evil.

"None but a lofty soul can feel the noble style of these *buffo* airs; they have neither the superabundant frivolity of Italian music nor the vulgar accent of French commonplace; rather have they the majesty of Olympus. There is the bitter laughter of a divine being mocking the surprise of a troubadour Don-Juanizing himself. But for this dignity we should be too suddenly brought down to the general tone of the opera, here stamped on that terrible fury of diminished sevenths which resolves itself into an infernal waltz, and finally brings us face to face with the demons.

"How emphatically Bertram's couplet stands out in B minor against that diabolical chorus, depicting his paternity, but mingling in fearful despair with these demoniacal strains.

"Then comes the delightful transition of Alice's reappearance, with the *ritornel* in B flat. I can still hear that air of angelical simplicity— the nightingale after a storm. Thus the grand leading idea of the whole is worked out in the details; for what could be more perfectly in contrast with the tumult of devils tossing in the pit than that wonderful air given to Alice? '*Quand j'ai quitte la Normandie.*'

"The golden thread of melody flows on, side by side with the mighty harmony, like a heavenly hope; it is embroidered on it, and with what marvelous skill! Genius never lets go of the science that guides it. Here Alice's song is in B flat leading into F sharp, the key of the demon's chorus. Do you hear the tremolo in the orchestra? The host of devils clamor for Robert.

"Bertram now reappears, and this is the culminating point of musical interest; after a *recitative*, worthy of comparison with the finest work of the great masters, comes the fierce conflict in E flat between two tremendous forces—one on the words '*Oui, tu me connais!*' on a diminished seventh; the other, on that sublime F, '*Le ciel est avec moi.*' Hell and the Crucifix have met for battle. Next we have Bertram threatening Alice, the most violent pathos ever heard—the Spirit of Evil expatiating complacently, and, as usual, appealing to personal interest. Robert's arrival gives us the magnificent unaccompanied trio in A flat, the first skirmish between the two rival forces and the man. And note how clearly that is expressed," said Gambara, epitomizing the scene with such passion of expression as startled Andrea.

"All this avalanche of music, from the clash of cymbals in common time, has been gathering up to this contest of three voices. The magic of evil triumphs! Alice flies, and you have the duet in D between Bertram and Robert. The devil sets his talons in the man's heart; he tears it to make it his own; he works on every feeling. Honor, hope, eternal and infinite pleasures—he displays them all. He places him, as he did Jesus, on the pinnacle of the Temple, and shows him all the treasures of the earth, the storehouse of sin. He nettles him to flaunt his courage; and the man's nobler mind is expressed in his exclamation:

"Des chevaliers de ma patrie
L'honneur toujours fut le soutien!

"And finally, to crown the work, the theme comes in which sounded the note of fatality at the beginning. Thus, the leading strain, the magnificent call to the deed:

"Nonnes qui reposez sous cette froide pierre,

Gambara

M'entendez-vous?

"The career of the music, gloriously worked out, is gloriously finished by the *allegro vivace* of the bacchanalian chorus in D minor. This, indeed, is the triumph of hell! Roll on, harmony, and wrap us in a thousand folds! Roll on, bewitch us! The powers of darkness have clutched their prey; they hold him while they dance. The great genius, born to conquer and to reign, is lost! The devils rejoice, misery stifles genius, passion will wreck the knight!"

And here Gambara improvised a *fantasia* of his own on the bacchanalian chorus, with ingenious variations, and humming the air in a melancholy drone as if to express the secret sufferings he had known.

"Do you hear the heavenly lamentations of neglected love?" he said. "Isabella calls to Robert above the grand chorus of knights riding forth to the tournament, in which the *motifs* of the second act reappear to make it clear that the third act has all taken place in a supernatural sphere. This is real life again. This chorus dies away at the approach of the hellish enchantment brought by Robert with the talisman. The deviltry of the third act is to be carried on. Here we have the duet with the viol; the rhythm is highly expressive of the brutal desires of a man who is omnipotent, and the Princess, by plaintive phrases, tries to win her lover back to moderation. The musician has here placed himself in a situation of great difficulty, and has surmounted it in the loveliest number of the whole opera. How charming is the melody of the *cavatina* 'Grace pour toi!' All the women present understood it well; each saw herself seized and snatched away on the stage. That part alone would suffice to make the fortune of the opera. Every woman felt herself engaged in a struggle with some violent lover. Never was music so passionate and so dramatic.

"The whole world now rises in arms against the reprobate. This *finale* may be criticised for its resemblance to that of *Don Giovanni*; but there is this immense difference: in Isabella we have the expression of the noblest faith, a true love that will save Robert, for he scornfully rejects the infernal powers bestowed on him, while Don Giovanni persists in his unbelief. Moreover, that particular fault is common to every composer who has written a *finale* since Mozart. The *finale* to *Don Giovanni* is one of those classic forms that are invented once for all.

"At last religion wins the day, uplifting the voice that governs worlds, that invites all sorrow to come for consolation, all repentance to be forgiven and helped.

"The whole house was stirred by the chorus:

> "Malheureaux on coupables
> Hatez-vous d'accourir!

"In the terrific tumult of raving passions, the holy Voice would have been unheard; but at this critical moment it sounds like thunder; the divine Catholic Church rises glorious in light. And here I was amazed to find that after such lavish use of harmonic treasure, the composer had come upon a new vein with the splendid chorus: '*Gloire a la Providence*' in the manner of Handel.

"Robert rushes on with his heartrending cry: '*Si je pouvais prier!*' and Bertram, driven by the infernal decree, pursues his son, and makes a last effort. Alice has called up the vision of the Mother, and now comes the grand trio to which the whole opera has led up: the triumph of the soul over matter, of the Spirit of Good over the Spirit of Evil. The strains of piety prevail over the chorus of hell, and happiness appears glorious; but here the music is weaker. I only saw a cathedral instead of hearing a concert of angels in bliss, and a divine prayer consecrating the union of Robert and Isabella. We ought not to have been left oppressed by the spells of hell; we ought to emerge with hope in our heart.

"I, as musician and a Catholic, wanted another prayer like that in *Mose*. I should have liked to see how Germany would contend with Italy, what Meyerbeer could do in rivalry with Rossini.

"However, in spite of this trifling blemish, the writer cannot say that after five hours of such solid music, a Parisian prefers a bit of ribbon to a musical masterpiece. You heard how the work was applauded; it will go through five hundred performances! If the French really understand that music—"

"It is because it expresses ideas," the Count put in.

"No; it is because it sets forth in a definite shape a picture of the struggle in which so many perish, and because every individual life is implicated in it through memory. Ah! I, hapless wretch, should have been too happy to hear the sound of those heavenly voices I have so often dreamed of."

Hereupon Gambara fell into a musical day-dream, improvising the most lovely melodious and harmonious *cavatina* that Andrea would ever hear on earth; a divine strain divinely performed on a theme as exquisite as that of *O filii et filioe*, but graced with additions such as none but the loftiest musical genius could devise.

The Count sat lost in keen admiration; the clouds cleared away, the blue sky opened, figures of angels appeared lifting the veil that hid the sanctuary, and the light of heaven poured down.

There was a sudden silence.

The Count, surprised at the cessation of the music, looked at Gambara, who, with fixed gaze, in the attitude of a visionary, murmured the word: "God!"

Andrea waited till the composer had descended from the enchanted realm to which he had soared on the many-hued wings of inspiration, intending to show him the truth by the light he himself would bring down with him.

"Well," said he, pouring him out another bumper of wine and clinking glasses with him, "this German has, you see, written a sublime opera without troubling himself with theories, while those musicians who write grammars of harmony may, like literary critics, be atrocious composers."

"Then you do not like my music?"

"I do not say so. But if, instead of carrying musical principles to an extreme—which takes you too far—you would simply try to arouse our feelings, you would be better understood, unless indeed you have mistaken your vocation. You are a great poet."

"What," cried Gambara, "are twenty-five years of study in vain? Am I to learn the imperfect language of men when I have the key to the heavenly tongue? Oh, if you are right,—I should die."

"No, no. You are great and strong; you would begin life again, and I would support you. We would show the world the noble and rare alliance of a rich man and an artist in perfect sympathy and understanding."

"Do you mean it?" asked Gambara, struck with amazement.

"As I have told you, you are a poet more than a musician."

"A poet, a poet! It is better than nothing. But tell me truly, which do you esteem most highly, Mozart or Homer?"

"I admire them equally."

"On your honor?"

"On my honor."

"H'm! Once more. What do you think of Meyerbeer and Byron?"

"You have measured them by naming them together."

The Count's carriage was waiting. The composer and his noble physician ran down-stairs, and in a few minutes they were with Marianna.

As they went in, Gambara threw himself into his wife's arms, but she drew back a step and turned away her head; the husband also drew back and beamed on the Count.

"Oh, monsieur!" said Gambara in a husky voice, "you might have left me my illusions." He hung his head, and then fell.

"What have you done to him? He is dead drunk!" cried Marianna, looking down at her husband with a mingled expression of pity and disgust.

The Count, with the help of his servant, picked up Gambara and laid him on his bed.

Then Andrea left, his heart exultant with horrible gladness.

The Count let the usual hour for calling slip past next day, for he began to fear lest he had duped himself and had made this humble couple pay too dear for their improved circumstances and added wisdom, since their peace was destroyed for ever.

At last Giardini came to him with a note from Marianna.

"Come," she wrote, "the mischief is not so great as you so cruelly meant it to be."

"Excellenza," said the cook, while Andrea was making ready, "you treated us splendidly last evening. But apart from the wine, which was excellent, your steward did not put anything on the table that was worthy to set before a true epicure. You will not deny, I suppose, that the dish I sent to you on the day when you did me the honor to sit down at my board, contained the quintessence of all those that disgraced your magnificent service of plate? And when I awoke this morning I remembered the promise you once made me of a place as *chef*. Henceforth I consider myself as a member of your household."

"I thought of the same thing a few days ago," replied Andrea. "I mentioned you to the secretary of the Austrian Embassy, and you have permission to recross the Alps as soon as you please. I have a castle in Croatia which I rarely visit. There you may combine the offices of gate-keeper, butler, and steward, with two hundred crowns a year. Your wife will have as much for doing all the rest of the work. You may make all the experiments you please *in anima vili*, that is to say on the stomach of my vassals. Here is a cheque for your traveling expenses."

Giardini kissed the Count's hand after the Neapolitan fashion.

"Excellenza," said he, "I accept the cheque, but beg to decline the place. It would dishonor me to give up my art by losing the opinion of the most perfect epicures, who are certainly to be found in Paris."

When Andrea arrived at Gambara's lodgings, the musician rose to welcome him.

"My generous friend," said he, with the utmost frankness, "you either took advantage, last evening, of the weakness of my brain to make a fool of me, or else your brain is no more capable of standing the test of the heady liquors of our native Latium, than mine is. I will assume this latter hypothesis; I would rather doubt your digestion

than your heart. Be this as it may, henceforth I drink no more wine—
for ever. The abuse of good liquor last evening led me into much
guilty folly. When I remember that I very nearly—" He gave a glance
of terror at Marianna. "As to the wretched opera you took me to
hear, I have thought it over, and it is, after all, music written on
ordinary lines, a mountain of piled-up notes, *verba et voces*. It is but
the dregs of the nectar I can drink in deep draughts as I reproduce
the heavenly music that I hear! It is a patchwork of airs of which I
could trace the origin. The passage '*Gloire a la Providence*' is too much
like a bit of Handel; the chorus of knights is closely related to the
Scotch air in *La Dame Blanche*; in short, if this opera is a success, it is
because the music is borrowed from everybody's—so it ought to be
popular.

"I will say good-bye to you, my dear friend. I have had some ideas
seething in my brain since the morning that only wait to soar up to
God on the wings of song, but I wished to see you. Good-bye; I must
ask forgiveness of the Muse. We shall meet at dinner to-night—but
no wine; at any rate, none for me. I am firmly resolved—"

"I give him up!" cried Andrea, flushing red.

"And you restore my sense of conscience," said Marianna. "I dared
not appeal to it! My friend, my friend, it is no fault of ours; he does
not want to be cured."

Six years after this, in January 1837, such artists as were so unlucky
as to damage their wind or stringed instruments, generally took
them to the Rue Froid-Manteau, to a squalid and horrible house,
where, on the fifth floor, dwelt an old Italian named Gambara.

For five years past he had been left to himself, deserted by his wife;
he had gone through many misfortunes. An instrument on which he
had relied to make his fortune, and which he called a *Panharmonicon*,
had been sold by order of the Court on the public square, Place du
Chatelet, together with a cartload of music paper scrawled with
notes. The day after the sale, these scores had served in the market to
wrap up butter, fish, and fruit.

Thus the three grand operas of which the poor man would boast, but
which an old Neapolitan cook, who was now but a patcher up of
broken meats, declared to be a heap of nonsense, were scattered

throughout Paris on the trucks of costermongers. But at any rate, the landlord had got his rent and the bailiffs their expenses.

According to the Neapolitan cook—who warmed up for the street-walkers of the Rue Froid-Manteau the fragments left from the most sumptuous dinners in Paris—Signora Gambara had gone off to Italy with a Milanese nobleman, and no one knew what had become of her. Worn out with fifteen years of misery, she was very likely ruining the Count by her extravagant luxury, for they were so devotedly adoring, that in all his life, Giardini could recall no instance of such a passion.

Towards the end of that very January, one evening when Giardini was chatting with a girl who had come to buy her supper, about the divine Marianna—so poor, so beautiful, so heroically devoted, and who had, nevertheless, "gone the way of them all," the cook, his wife, and the street-girl saw coming towards them a woman fearfully thin, with a sunburned, dusty face; a nervous walking skeleton, looking at the numbers, and trying to recognize a house.

"*Ecco la Marianna!*" exclaimed the cook.

Marianna recognized Giardini, the erewhile cook, in the poor fellow she saw, without wondering by what series of disasters he had sunk to keep a miserable shop for secondhand food. She went in and sat down, for she had come from Fontainebleau. She had walked fourteen leagues that day, after begging her bread from Turin to Paris.

She frightened that terrible trio! Of all her wondrous beauty nothing remained but her fine eyes, dimmed and sunken. The only thing faithful to her was misfortune.

She was welcomed by the skilled old instrument mender, who greeted her with unspeakable joy.

"Why, here you are, my poor Marianna!" said he, warmly. "During your absence they sold up my instrument and my operas."

It would have been difficult to kill the fatted calf for the return of the Samaritan, but Giardini contributed the fag end of a salmon, the trull paid for wine, Gambara produced some bread, Signora Giardini lent a cloth, and the unfortunates all supped together in the musician's garret.

When questioned as to her adventures, Marianna would make no reply; she only raised her beautiful eyes to heaven and whispered to Giardini:

"He married a dancer!"

"And how do you mean to live?" said the girl. "The journey has ruined you, and—"

"And made me an old woman," said Marianna. "No, that is not the result of fatigue or hardship, but of grief."

"And why did you never send your man here any money?" asked the girl.

Marianna's only answer was a look, but it went to the woman's heart.

"She is proud with a vengeance!" she exclaimed. "And much good it has done her!" she added in Giardini's ear.

All that year musicians took especial care of their instruments, and repairs did not bring in enough to enable the poor couple to pay their way; the wife, too, did not earn much by her needle, and they were compelled to turn their talents to account in the lowest form of employment. They would go out together in the dark to the Champs Elysees and sing duets, which Gambara, poor fellow, accompanied on a wretched guitar. On the way, Marianna, who on these expeditions covered her head with a sort of veil of coarse muslin, would take her husband to the grocer's shop in the Faubourg Saint-Honore and give him two or three thimblefuls of brandy to make him tipsy; otherwise he could not play. Then they would stand up together in front of the smart people sitting on the chairs, and one of the greatest geniuses of the time, the unrecognized Orpheus of Modern Music, would perform passages from his operas—pieces so remarkable that they would extract a few half-pence from Parisian supineness. When some *dilettante* of comic operas happened to be sitting there and did not recognize from what work they were taken, he would question the woman dressed like a Greek priestess, who held out a bottle-stand of stamped metal in which she collected charity.

"I say, my dear, what is that music out of?"

"The opera of *Mahomet*," Marianna would reply.

As Rossini composed an opera called *Mahomet II.*, the amateur would say to his wife, sitting at his side:

"What a pity it is that they will never give us at the Italiens any operas by Rossini but those we know. That is really fine music!"

And Gambara would smile.

Only a few days since, this unhappy couple had to pay the trifling sum of thirty-six francs as arrears for rent for the cock-loft in which they lived resigned. The grocer would not give them credit for the brandy with which Marianna plied her husband to enable him to play. Gambara was, consequently, so unendurably bad that the ears of the wealthy were irresponsive, and the tin bottle-stand remained empty.

It was nine o'clock in the evening. A handsome Italian, the Principessa Massimilla De Varese, took pity on the poor creatures; she gave them forty francs and questioned them, discerning from the woman's thanks that she was a Venetian. Prince Emilio would know the history of their woes, and Marianna told it, making no complaints of God or men.

"Madame," said Gambara, as she ended, for he was sober, "we are victims of our own superiority. My music is good. But as soon as music transcends feeling and becomes an idea, only persons of genius should be the hearers, for they alone are capable of responding to it! It is my misfortune that I have heard the chorus of angels, and believed that men could understand the strains. The same thing happens to women when their love assumes a divine aspect: men cannot understand them."

This speech was well worth the forty francs bestowed by Massimilla; she took out a second gold piece, and told Marianna she would write to Andrea Marcosini.

"Do not write to him, madame!" exclaimed Marianna. "And God grant you to always be beautiful!"

"Let us provide for them," said the Princess to her husband; "for this man has remained faithful to the Ideal which we have killed."

As he saw the gold pieces, Gambara shed tears; and then a vague reminiscence of old scientific experiments crossed his mind, and the hapless composer, as he wiped his eyes, spoke these words, which the circumstances made pathetic:

"Water is a product of burning."

PARIS, June 1837.

ADDENDUM

The following personages appear in other stories of the Human Comedy.

Varese, Emilio Memmi, Prince of
 Massimilla Doni

Varese, Princess of
 Massimilla Doni